# HYENA ROAD

*Based on the Screenplay by Paul Gross*

HarperCollins*PublishersLtd*

*This story is dedicated to the men and women*
*of the Canadian Forces—*
*those who have served and those who will*

*

*Hyena Road*
Novelization based on the screenplay by Paul Gross.
Copyright © 2015 by HarperCollins Publishers Ltd.
All rights reserved.

Published by HarperCollins Publishers Ltd

First edition

HarperCollins books may be purchased for educational, business,
or sales promotional use through our Special Markets Department.

HarperCollins Publishers Ltd
2 Bloor Street East, 20th Floor
Toronto, Ontario, Canada, M4W 1A8

*www.harpercollins.ca*

Library and Archives Canada Cataloguing in Publication
information is available upon request

ISBN 978-1-44344-708-9

Printed and bound in the United States of America
OPM 9 8 7 6 5 4 3 2 1

# Glossary of Military Terms

| | |
|---|---|
| A-10 | close air support attack aircraft |
| AK | AK-47, an enemy assault rifle |
| ANA | Afghan National Army |
| ANP | Afghan National Police |
| AO | area of operations |
| ASI | Call source intelligence centre |
| BDA | battle damage assessment |
| C7 | Canadian assault rifle |
| C8 | smaller, carbine variant of the C7 |
| C15 Tac-50 | Canadian long-range sniper rifle |
| C-130 | transport plane |
| Chinook | heavy-lift helicopter |
| CIMIC | civil-military cooperation |
| CLP | combat logistics patrol |
| Coyote | .308 rifle |
| CP | command post |
| det | detachment; also detonator |
| DFAC | dining facility, or mess |
| effects | a type of military planning that combines lethal and non-lethal missions in order to contribute to the overall operation |
| EOD | explosives ordnance disposal |
| Griffon | transport helicopter |
| IED | improvised explosive device |

| | |
|---|---|
| IMP | individual meal pack, or field ration |
| ISAF | International Security Assistance Force |
| KAF | Kandahar Airfield |
| KIA | killed in action |
| LAV | light armoured vehicle |
| locstat | location statement |
| LZ | landing zone |
| MBITR | multiband inter/intra-team radio |
| mikes | minutes |
| OC | officer commanding |
| OP | observation post |
| PT | physical training, working out |
| PTT | press-to-talk function on a radio |
| QRF | quick reaction force |
| Raufoss | an armour-piercing round |
| RG-31 | multi-purpose, mine-resistant patrol vehicle |
| RMC | Royal Military College of Canada |
| RPG | rocket-propelled grenade |
| RV | rendezvous; also Romeo-Victor |
| sitrep | situation report |
| TIC | troops in contact |
| TOC | tactical operations centre |
| UAV | unmanned aerial vehicle, or drone |
| VBIED | vehicle-borne improvised explosive device |
| warning order | formal document that precedes an operation order and starts subordinate planning and preparation |

# HYENA ROAD

# 1

THE STRANGEST DAY OF Warrant Officer Ryan Murphy's time in Afghanistan was the day he met the old man called the Ghost. That day, and that encounter, set the turbulent pace for everything that followed.

The day began normally, with a target engagement along a lonely stretch of Hyena Road several kilometres east of Sperwan Ghar. Engagements of some kind or another on Hyena Road were an almost daily occurrence. The insurgents were not happy about the long stretch of new hardtop. That day, a man had appeared just after first light broke in the east. It was the same time the Adhan would be sounding from the muezzins, but there were no muezzins out here. Out here there were only the dirt, the rocks, the stunted brushwood, and the empty grape fields. Hyena Road was the only sign of the modern world cutting through this brown-grey landscape. A naked mountain reared against the horizon.

At first the man was only a flutter of movement; his loose-fitting shalwar kameez and dark vest and *pakul* might have been indistinguishable from the pre-dawn wasteland around him had he appeared ten minutes before. A canvas satchel, weighted with something heavy, was slung over his back.

The man stopped at a point in the roadside where a large notch—loosely remediated with sand and gravel—cut a metre from the shoulder into the new but crude hardtop. He squatted down and unslung his satchel and set it carefully behind him. Then he started digging with his hands through the gravel. His motions were oddly doglike.

At more than half a kilometre's distance, framed inside the spotter's scope, no sound accompanied the digging man. The effect was surreal. Ryan watched for five full seconds. Then he thumbed the PTT switch on his MBITR and softly said, "Three Niner Alpha, this is Six-Six. Contact. Grid Quebec Quebec 4176 8134. One times civilian, he's wearing grey man jams, black vest, black headdress. Looks like he's digging by the side of the road. We're observing from 650 metres south-southwest of him. Wait out."

A moment passed, and then the reply crackled through his headset, the volume turned very low: "Three Niner Alpha, roger."

Jenn, thought Ryan. Immediately he suppressed the thought. She wasn't Jenn right now. She was Captain Bowman, Charlie Company second-in-command. At present, the company commander, Major Shaw, was on leave. That left Jenn in charge. She was Six-Six's lifeline out here in bandit country.

Ryan looked back through the spotter's scope. The man by the notch in the roadside was still clawing at the dirt and gravel. What the man was doing was weird, but this was a country of weirdness. There wasn't anything wrong with the man. Yet.

Ryan moved his head back from the scope. The muscles in his neck and shoulders were very stiff— he'd been lying prone and mostly motionless for a few hours now, simply observing. He looked at the dim readout on his wind meter. His field message pad was set in the dirt beside the base of his scope. He flipped the pages until he came to a laminated chart, no bigger than a playing card.

"Gusts at fifteen to fifty," he murmured. "Deflection one point five."

Close beside Ryan was Master Corporal Travis Davidson, also prone, manning the C15 Tac-50. Travis reached his left hand up from the stock to the scope on the top of the rifle—his right hand never strayed from the pistol-grip and trigger—and adjusted the reticle. He whispered, "Roger all. Standby. Nothing much to—wait, buddy's got something."

Ryan quickly put his eye back to the spotter's scope. Half a klick away the man by the roadside had pulled something out of the dirt. It was long and thin. A stick, maybe, or a pipe?

"A shovel," said Travis.

Ryan watched through the scope. The man held the shovel upright for a moment. The blade on the end was rusted and dented but clearly visible. Then the man set it on the ground beside him. He still hadn't straightened up from his squatting position.

Ryan had two other snipers—Tank and

Hickey—nearby, covering local security. He flipped his comms to the intra-det channel and gave them a quick update on what was happening.

"Could be a farmer," came Hickey's voice.

"Farming the side of the road?" said Ryan.

"Hey, Warrant, it's the 'Stan," said Hickey. "As soon as you got these people figured out, you let me know."

Ryan smiled and flipped his comms back to the company net. He watched as the man on the roadside rotated his torso and reached into the satchel he'd brought with him. Then the man turned his body back around. In his hands was an oblong metal object. The satchel lay limp and empty behind him.

"Shell casing," said Ryan. "122 millimetre."

"Bad move," said Travis. "See the cord?"

Ryan squinted. A thin strand of yellow detonator cord hung in a loop from the bottom of the shell. At this distance, in the faint light, the cord was almost invisible, even through the scope. Ryan thumbed his comms. "Three Niner Alpha, this is Six-Six. Sitrep on contact. I have positive ID on one times insurgent. He's got an IED, appears to be a 122-millimetre shell casing with det cord emanating from the base. Time of contact zero six twelve hours. I'm observing. Wait out."

Her voice crackled back immediately" "Six-six, this is Three Niner Alpha. Acknowledged. *Emanating?*"

There was no difference in her tone but he could picture her smiling. A smile crossed his own cracked and dry lips. The conflicting thoughts came to him again. She was Captain Bowman, bent over the battle board in the CP back at Sper. But she was also Jennifer, Jenn, in a seaside hotel room in Cyprus—

"Buddy's putting the projectile in the hole," said Travis.

Ryan observed. Their target already had the shell casing embedded in the hole he'd taken the shovel from. "Three Niner Alpha, this is Six-Six," Ryan said. "He's digging the device into the ground. We are going to engage. Will advise."

"Three Niner Alpha," she came back. "Acknowledged."

"Wait till he stands back up," Ryan said to Travis. "Then engage. On."

"Standing by," said Travis. He brought his thumb up from the pistol-grip and pushed the

safety lever forward. It was an almost imperceptible motion. Then he settled his finger against
the curve of the trigger.

The man by the side of the road straightened
up. He had the shovel in one hand and the yellow
detonator cord in the other. He looked left, then
right. At that moment the first rays of the sun
broke out over the austere land.

"Send it," said Ryan.

Travis pulled the trigger. The rifle thundered.
There was a second's delay, and then Ryan could
see a red-black hole open in the middle of the
man's chest as the .50-calibre round slammed
through him. The man's arms shot out to his sides.
He dropped first to his knees, as if in prayer, then
slumped over. His left leg kicked in the gravel.
Blood was already pooling around him, glittering
in the lean reach of the sun. The rifle shot was still
echoing out in all directions.

Ryan observed for a count of three. The man's
leg slowed its kicking, then stopped.

"Three Niner Alpha, Six-Six," said Ryan.

"Three Niner Alpha, send."

"Six-Six. One times insurgent engaged in
centre mass. No motion. Over."

"Three Niner Alpha. Roger that, Six-Six. One times insurgent KIA. We'll push higher assets to conduct the BDA."

"Six-Six acknowledged," said Ryan. The sound of the gunshot had given away their position, and they would have to move out as soon as they could. "It's a soft compromise on our position. We're going to pack up and move to Romeo-Victor for extraction at Quebec Quebec 4199 8226."

"Three Niner Alpha, roger," said Jennifer. "Your ride will be en route, over."

"Six-Six exfilling now," said Ryan. "Out."

Travis was already collapsing the bipod on the Tac-50. He said, "I'll bring in Hickey and Tank."

Ryan nodded, closing the cover over the eyepiece on the spotter's scope. He didn't know if anyone—particularly any Taliban—had heard the shot, but Six-Six's only job that day was to observe their designated stretch of road and put down any bombers. With that finished, the task at hand now was to get his boys out in one piece.

Within five minutes Six-Six had collapsed their hide. Nobody said anything. They didn't need to. This was a drill they'd practised countless times before.

A man's voice crackled over Ryan's headset: "Six-Six, this is Three One Charlie. We're on the move. We'll see you at the Romeo-Victor. Over."

"Three One Charlie, Six-Six," said Ryan. "See you there. Out."

Three One Charlie was the patrol coming to get them. Four LAVs. Ryan was never really comfortable riding as a passenger in a LAV— they were too vulnerable to IEDs—but it would have otherwise been a long hump back to Sper on foot, with their rucks and vests and plates and weapons. He briefly thought about a meal in the mess tent. A shower. A snooze. Jenn. He also thought about the man on the road. Anyone within a few kilometres would have heard the shot from the Tac-50, but not the man they'd been targeting. He'd been dead long before the sound had reached his position. He hadn't even known what was coming. Life in one instant, nothingness the next.

Ryan hoisted his ruck onto his back and slung his C8 across his chest. It was time to get moving.

- - -

Six-Six's designated extraction RV was on Hyena Road, a fairly short distance west of where they'd established their hide. But they couldn't follow the road itself; it was too open, too visible. Instead, they would need to track cross-country, staying stealthy, using the cover of the landscape. Ryan had mapped out a route that doglegged first to the south, through the grape fields, and then northwest, over a small goat path between two rocky high crags. The route was a little over two kilometres all told. He estimated they could do it in under an hour—assuming there were no setbacks.

They made their way south in single file, a few metres between each man. Hickey was on point, Ryan pacing their steps behind him, Tank coming third, and Travis in the rear. The sun was still low enough that most of what Ryan could see was little more than shadow or silhouette.

Underfoot, the earth was colourless and gritty, banked up into long, waist-high windrows by decades or centuries or more of grape farming. At this time of year the vines between the windrows were mostly barren. It was early June and the grapes had only just begun to grow back. In Afghanistan, farming and fighting were inextricably linked: during the fall and winter, the insurgents tended to go home to tend their crops and bring in their harvests; in early summer, as the new crops began to come in, the insurgents would take up their arms again.

Ryan was compelled to think again about the man they'd engaged on Hyena Road, the man who never heard the shot coming. Had that man sowed seeds as readily as he'd buried—or tried to, anyway—bombs by the side of the road? And wasn't there a Bible passage about turning swords into ploughs or something like that? Trav would know, Ryan thought.

Of course, grapes weren't the only thing that was harvested around here. These grape fields could also conceal broad stands of poppies. From the poppies came opium. Opium was an incomparable fortune in the hands of whoever controlled it—Taliban and crooked local power broker alike. As the daylight increased, Ryan kept his eyes open for the telltale pink blossoms that would stand out against the brown and green. It wouldn't be the first time a stand of poppies had been discovered, and subsequently razed, on this part of the map.

A short distance farther along, Ryan called a halt. They'd come to a dry creek bed running along the edge of the grape field. Each man in the det took a knee, forming a rough circle, and kept silent observation to his front and sides. Ryan briefly consulted his map. They were three hundred metres north of a small village named on the map as Haji Baba; in the middle distance, he could just make out the top of the rough-hewn mud-brick wall encircling the village.

Ryan—and Travis and Tank and Hickey—had been down here before. Six-Six had conducted an overwatch operation on the far side of the village a few months ago. That was during the early days of this deployment, before Hyena Road had been constructed. Six-Six had observed a small number of insurgents moving through a poppy field outside the village. They'd called in the contact and then watched as an artillery strike blew those men, whoever they were, to pieces. Quick and easy. Ryan wondered if there was a square inch of this land that hadn't had blood soaked into it at one time or other.

In any case, this was as far south as they were going today. From here they would head northwest, over the goat path between the crags, and meet their extraction.

He clicked on his radio and sent their location to the CP. Jennifer's voice came back: "Six-Six, this is Three Niner Alpha. Your locstat is acknowledged. Your ride is approximately thirty mikes out, over."

"Six-Six, roger," said Ryan. "Thirty mikes is about what we'll need. Out."

A moment later the det was on the move again, in the same single file as before, the rocky crags getting ever nearer. Hot coffee and breakfast in an hour, Ryan thought. An hour and a half at most.

- - -

They made much better time to the goat path than Ryan had estimated, covering the distance in a little less than twenty minutes. Up the path they went, scrabbling over loose rock, clinging to boulders and ledges, each man by now feeling the full weight of his kit and starting to sweat through his combats. Behind them, the lowland they'd moved through was washed by bright early-morning sunlight, scant green foliage fighting through the ever-present brown. The dozen adobe buildings of Haji Baba were visible through the thin mist rising up from the earth. In the furthest distance the rust-coloured plateaus of the Registan marked the horizon from west to east. The vista, for all its ancient severity, was oddly beautiful.

Ryan checked in with their LAV escort. It was still ten minutes to the west. Ryan nodded. He took over point from Hickey and proceeded to the rounded summit of the goat path, flanked by the crags on either side. Here, looking north, he could almost see the whole of Panjwayi District before him. More green struggling against the brown, tiny villages here and there, and almost at the limit of vision, the hazy outskirts of Kandahar City.

Immediately below them, no more than a hundred metres away, was the stretch of Hyena Road they'd designated as the RV with their escorts. There was no one in sight, man or animal. No breeze, no sound. Ryan started to lead the descent.

He called a short halt halfway. The three others took up positions behind him, crouching behind boulders and ledges and fallen rocks. Ryan blinked sweat out of his eyes. He brought up his C8 and scanned the road through the optical sight. He scanned a hundred metres to the west, where a narrow concrete culvert undercut the hardtop, and then a hundred metres to the east. Nothing. Only a few minutes until the LAVs arrived, he reckoned.

He gestured for the det to resume its descent. He heard the quiet sounds of the snipers getting to their feet behind him. Ryan himself took one step.

He stopped.

He lowered himself first to his knee and then leaned back so that his ruck was braced against the downslope behind him. This was a steadier posture. He laid the forward grip of his C8 over his knee and looked through the sight again.

There was a light skittering of pebbles. It was Trav, carefully sliding into place beside Ryan. "What's up?" Travis whispered.

"Spidey senses," said Ryan. "See that culvert?"

Travis looked through the optical sight on his C8. "Different colour in the road."

"Yeah," said Ryan.

"Shit. A couple places."

Ryan looked through his sight again. There was one small patch of hardtop a little darker than the tarmac around it. He'd noticed that patch but only that patch. As he studied the area he saw that Travis was right—there was more than one patch. There were five, spread out over a stretch of thirty or forty metres. On the other side of the road, a hundred metres up through an empty field, was a jumble of stones that might once have been a wall.

"Could be somebody lost their oil pan," said Travis.

"Could be," said Ryan. He flipped on his comms. "Three One Charlie, this is Six-Six. What's your ETA?"

The voice of the patrol commander came back: "Six-Six, Three One Charlie. We're about three or four minutes, other side of the hill."

"Three One Charlie, Six-Six," said Ryan. "I advise you hold your position. Do not come around the high feature. I say again, do not come around the high feature. We've got something weird on the road. Gonna have a look. Wait out."

"Three One Charlie, good copy," said the LAV commander.

Ryan let go of his comms. He studied the road a moment longer. He gestured at the rock pile in the empty field beyond the road. "If you were a triggerman or a spotter . . ."

"That'd be a good place to watch from," said Travis. "We *could* request EOD."

"We could. Long wait."

"Long wait," Travis agreed.

"Hickey?" said Ryan. "Get the Coyote on one of those oil stains over the culvert. Put a round in it."

Another moment elapsed as Hickey laid his rifle across a boulder and sighted. He fired. The report of the .308 was not as huge as the Tac-50's but it still made a sharp crack in the still air. Ryan, watching through his sight, saw a puff of dust rise up from one of the patches on the road. Nothing happened. The echoes of the rifle shot receded and the silence that followed was eerie. Ryan swung his sight up to the rock pile. For a brief instant he thought he saw a flash of light— reflection on binoculars?—but it was gone before he could be sure.

"What do you think?" said Ryan.

"It's probably nothing," said Travis. "I think it's just bad road."

"What if you're wrong?"

"Have I ever been wrong?" said Travis.

Ryan smiled. He did not take his eyes off the

tarmac. He said, "Hickey, just for fun? Chamber up a Raufoss."

Ryan could hear as Hickey dug around in his kit, finding himself an incendiary round, staying as quiet as he could. Then there were the sounds of Hickey working the bolt on his rifle. A moment later, he said, "Standing by."

Ryan inhaled and exhaled. "Send it," he said.

The Coyote cracked again. Through his sight, Ryan caught a short glimpse of a small chunk of tarmac being dislodged—and then the explosion came. The hardtop heaved up and split and a tremendous mass of dust and smoke mushroomed into the air. The sound of it was not so much heard as felt, a powerful open-handed blow against Ryan's chest and throat and eardrums. If he weren't already propped on his ruck he would've been knocked off his feet. Bits of debris were raining down around him.

Ryan checked himself over. As far as he could tell he was intact. "Everybody good?" he called.

Before anyone could reply, Travis said, "Ambush." He said it calmly, as if he were remarking on the weather.

Ryan looked through his sight at the far side

of the road. He saw men rising out of the ruts and ditches in the empty field. Six—no, seven, eight, *nine*—of them. Dark, loose-fitting clothes, black turbans, one or two of them wearing tactical vests, all of them armed with AKs. Ryan brought his rifle back to the rock pile, and this time there was no doubt. The sunlight was reflecting brightly off the binoculars of the man who'd halfway risen up from behind the rocks. The man who was looking directly at Six-Six.

Ryan, still with his C8 braced over his knee, took half a second to steady his breathing. With his thumb he flipped off the safety. His finger tightened on the trigger. The range was a little over two hundred metres. Easy, even with a short-barrelled carbine. The sound of the gunshot was flat and atonal. Through the sight he saw the binoculars drop as the spotter's head snapped back.

"We're blown," said Travis, still in that calm tone.

"Let's move," Ryan called. "Back over the ridge."

"Covering," said Tank. "Go!"

Tank and Hickey put covering fire into the field across the road, Tank firing short bursts with his C8 and Hickey taking aimed shots with the

Coyote, as Ryan and Travis pulled themselves off the downslope, spun around, and doubled back up to the summit where the goat path cut through the crags. Dirt and pebbles kicked up around them. It was return fire going wide, but return fire all the same.

Ryan thumbed his comms. "Three Niner Alpha, this is Six-Six. Sitrep. We are being effectively engaged. We are backtracking from our present location. Over."

Jennifer came back: "Three Niner Alpha, roger. Three One Charlie, can you get in there and assist?"

The voice of the LAV commander crackled back: "Three One Charlie, roger that. Moving out now."

"Three One Charlie, this is Six-Six," said Ryan. "Negative. Do not come around the high feature. The road is filled with IEDs. You're the target. Can you circle back, meet us east of here?"

There was a slight pause, then the LAV commander came back: "Three One Charlie. Roger, but we'll need to get turned around—"

"Break break," Jennifer interrupted. "Six-Six, Three Niner Alpha. What's the enemy force size?"

Ryan took a glance back at the field below.

There was more movement. Much more than he'd seen already. Over the distance and the gunfire he could dimly make out a voice yelling commands in Pashto.

"Six-Six," said Ryan. "I estimate two zero hostiles. Maybe more. We're moving now. Wait out."

*Twenty* Taliban, he thought. At least twenty. Incredible. The LAVs were the target, but Six-Six had sprung the trap. Now they were outnumbered five to one. From the summit he and Travis laid down covering fire with their C8s. Hickey and Tank bounded up and past them and started the descent on the far side. Ryan and Travis fell in behind.

Coming up this way ten minutes earlier had been steep and challenging; going down this same way, at speed, could be disastrous if they lost their footing. The snipers slid and scrambled on the loose grit of the hillside, keeping one hand on their weapons and using the other hand to grab at anything that would arrest their descent. If one of them broke a leg out here they would all be in bad trouble.

Ryan took the lead, angling their descent laterally across the slope. It was about three hundred metres to the far side of the high feature. Another hundred metres through the low-lying grape fields to the road. The LAVs could bound forward firing, if necessary—

Ryan lost his footing. He didn't pitch forward but he did drop onto his ass. A jolt of pain shot up from his tailbone, and his ruck bashed roughly against his shoulders and neck. He slid forward another ten paces, to the bottom of the hill, and fetched up in a shallow gulch beside a dense snarl of grapevines.

Travis skidded to a halt beside him and hauled Ryan to his feet. Ryan's entire back, from his ankles to the base of his skull, was throbbing, but he didn't think anything was broken. Tank and Hickey scooted into the gulch a few seconds later.

For the moment there was no gunfire. Then, out of sight—but not far away—came the sound of the Pashto commands again.

"They got us cut off," Tank whispered hoarsely. "I saw them coming around the high feature. Eight or nine at least, moving south."

"If we try to go west we'll be right on top of them," said Travis.

"Is there anything even remotely gay about this situation?" muttered Hickey.

"Yeah," said Tank. "You are, honey."

Ryan's mind worked quickly. If they kept moving west they'd be right into the line of Taliban Tank had seen coming around the base of the high feature. Ryan also had to assume there were insurgents coming around the other side of the high feature as well, working Six-Six into the middle of a pincer manoeuvre. So west and east were both ruled out. So was north. He thought about the operation they'd done overwatch on a few months ago. That village. Haji Baba. He worked spit into his mouth. "We'll go south. Hole up in the village until we can get hard extraction. I'll take point. Let's move."

---

It wasn't quite seven-thirty in the morning and already the heat was hellish. Six-Six moved in single file, staying low, down a windrow through the grape fields outside Haji Baba. Each sniper was too weighted down with his weapons and vest and helmet and kit for an all-out sprint; the best they could manage was a steady, ponderous jog. Each breath felt dry and roasted. They hadn't heard the Pashto commands in two or three minutes, but that didn't mean Six-Six had been forgotten.

Another minute of jogging and they came to the edge of the broad, grassy tract between the grape fields and Haji Baba. The mud-brick curtain wall around the village was inscrutable, pale in the sunlight.

Jennifer's voice crackled across Ryan's headset: "Six-Six, Three Niner Alpha. Send sitrep."

"Six-Six," said Ryan. "We are still in contact. We cannot Romeo-Victor with Three One Charlie from our present location—enemy has us cut off. We're moving to a village, reference Haji Baba, and will strongpoint from there and send grid. Over."

"Three Niner Alpha, acknowledged. I'm working with higher means to coordinate support. Will advise."

The higher means Jenn was referring to was the battle group. She'd be working through them to get fast air, artillery, or anything else that could be thrown Six-Six's way. The battle-group operations officer was a major named Lavigne, a level-headed

Quebecker who would be quick to help. Ryan felt a slight twinge of hope.

At the same time, it occurred to Ryan how Jenn's voice sounded steady and professional, almost that same level of calm as Travis had. He could hear a tremor in it, barely perceptible but there all the same. He wondered if the same tiny tremor sounded through his own voice.

Before they crossed into the open ground, each sniper took a moment to change out the magazine in his weapon. They had each left Sper with ten magazines and another two hundred rounds of clipped ammunition, plus frag and smoke grenades, plus sidearms, but if they had to strongpoint against a committed enemy their ammo wouldn't last long.

"Straight across the open ground to the wall, then up and over," said Ryan. "Hickey and Tank first. Move now."

Hickey went first and Tank followed, a few paces behind. When they'd covered half the distance, Ryan slapped Travis on the arm and Travis bounded forward. Ryan himself was last. The mud-brick wall bounced in his vision, at once getting closer and at the same time remaining impossibly far away. He sucked at the hot air. The weight of his kit felt as if it had doubled, and sweat was pouring into his eyes. He had a sudden memory of being a kid, no more than eight or nine, sprinting between third base and home plate in a game of pickup baseball on a summer afternoon.

At last Ryan skidded to a halt at the wall. Travis and Tank and Hickey were already spaced out along it. The wall was too high to get over here, but a short distance away a shallow notch had been knocked out of the bricks to make room for the limbs of a willow tree. Ryan pointed. The snipers started to make their move.

A sudden burst of automatic fire came from the grape fields. Small chunks of adobe kicked off the wall near Travis's head. Trav did a half-turn and fired a burst in return. Ryan looked and saw three Taliban making a quick lateral move, each man well-spaced from the next, across the edge of the field. Ryan let off a burst of his own. Dirt and dust lifted from the earth around his targets. The Taliban disappeared behind a windrow. A voice rose in Pashto.

At the notch in the wall Hickey was already up

and over. Tank was next, moving with adrenaline-fuelled agility. As soon as the top of Tank's helmet was out of sight, Travis scrambled lithely up. Last was Ryan. He let his C8 drop into its sling across his chest and he jumped and grabbed at the edges of the notch. A single bullet smashed into the wall half a metre away. Another passed through the air above him. He could plainly hear the whip-crack noise it made. For one giddy second his boots could not seem to get purchase on the mud bricks. His hands threatened to lose their grip. Then Tank appeared, catching hold of Ryan's wrists and hauling him over just as three or four more rounds cut through the air overhead.

- - -

Six-Six had a minute, two at most, to collect themselves on the other side of the wall. Each sniper checked himself over. Hickey had rolled his ankle and Ryan's back still hurt, but that was the worst they'd suffered. No gunshot wounds so far. Ryan took quick stock of their new location. They'd landed in an alley between two mud-brick buildings. What he could see of Haji Baba, so far, was devoid of any pattern of life. Rickety wooden doors were closed fast and shutters were pulled over the windows. It seemed like the village was deserted, but of course it wasn't. The locals were just holed up, hiding. Through the nooks and crannies, Six-Six was being watched. Ryan could feel it as tangibly as he could feel the heat of the day.

At that moment there was a burst of speculative AK fire from beyond the wall. One voice rose in Pashto, then another voice, then a third. The voices all sounded some distance away, maybe a hundred metres, but they were each coming from different directions.

"Fuckers are circling the village," muttered Hickey.

Ryan nodded. "These houses won't work for strongpoints," he said, keeping his voice low. "We need a compound with a wall. Fall in, boys. Tank, you got the rear, I've got eyes front. Let's move."

As they stepped off, Jennifer's voice came over the comms: "Six-Six, Three Niner Alpha. Zero is pushing fast air your way but you're going to have to hang in there."

"Six-Six acknowledged," said Ryan. "We're

in the village, finding a strongpoint. Will advise. Out."

He led his team down the alley. They worked their way around a corner and came out into an opening that passed for the village square. There was a squat concrete pad with a pump sticking out of it. There were three shops with thatched awnings, all three closed behind rusty metal roll-down doors. A lone goat, tied to a wooden post, eyed the snipers.

On the far side of the square was another mud-brick wall, this one with a set of pale-blue wooden doors in it. Ryan could see a two-storey adobe building rising above the compound wall. He made straight for the doors.

AK fire cracked out from nearby—definitely inside the village now. There was another forceful holler in Pashto.

Ryan arrived at the doors in the compound wall. He shot his boot into the wood. The doors clapped inward. Ryan pivoted away, his back to the doorframe, covering his det as they filed past him into the compound. He watched the square overtop of his C8 sight. The only thing moving was the goat, but he could sense the insurgents closing in. Travis passed Ryan through the doorway. Ryan fell in behind. He kicked the doors shut again as soon as he'd passed inside.

The courtyard inside the compound wall was dusty and drab. The two-storey building was a solid-looking block against the back of the compound. There were three or four smaller outbuildings, all built out from the wall. A couple of metal fuel drums were stacked in one corner. A yellow jug of cooking oil stood next to a hand pump. Some chickens were scratching in the dirt. More than that, there were three women—fully cloaked in blue burqas—and six children in miniature shalwar kameez, all staring at the snipers.

Travis put his right hand on his chest and said, "Salaam alaikum."

As if the words were a cue, the women and children scattered, making for the main building and smaller structures.

The dust of the hasty departure hung in the air for a moment, and when it settled, an old man was revealed. He was tall and thin, but his posture was ramrod straight. Proud. His robes were plain. A well-worn *shemagh* was draped around his neck and a simple turban was wrapped around his head. Above the thick grey fringe of his beard, he had a deeply lined face that looked as if it had been carved out of hardwood. Most striking of all were his eyes: one dark brown, the other pale blue.

Another man appeared. Ryan hadn't noticed him. This new man, dressed in off-white garments, had a face that was markedly similar to the old man's but much softer with youth. The younger man was holding a child in each of his arms. They were both girls, no older than eight, in bright red clothing and shawls. Their small, wide-eyed faces were delicately beautiful, all the more so against their grim surroundings.

The young man spoke to the elder. The young man kept his voice quiet, but his thinly contained alarm was clearly audible. The elder, not once taking his eyes off Ryan's, simply nodded. He spoke a few words in reply. He was quiet as well, but he did not sound disconcerted whatsoever.

The young man nodded and hurried over to the main building, still holding the little girls in the crook of each arm. He disappeared into the shadows beyond the narrow doorway.

Ryan put his hand to his chest. "Salaam—"

A small round object popped over the compound wall and thumped down into the dust between Ryan and the elder.

In the half-second it took for Ryan to register what the object was, the old man had bent over and picked the grenade up and tossed it back over the wall. A half-second after that came the heavy crump of the thing detonating. Two angry voices followed, as did another burst of AK fire.

"Is he asking us in?" said Hickey.

The old man was gesturing at the dark doorway of the main building.

"I think he's trying to help us," said Travis.

Two more bursts of gunfire. They could hear rounds striking the other side of the compound wall. The bullets likely wouldn't penetrate, but if the insurgents out there had an RPG . . .

Ryan nodded at the old man and bounded forward, through the doorway. If this was some kind of trap, he would spring it himself before his det got caught in it.

But there was no trap. There was a dim, low-ceilinged main room with carpets on the dirt floor and a thick smell of cooking oil and woodsmoke in the air. Then there were Travis and

Hickey and Tank, piling in behind Ryan. Last came the old man, following his guests into the house.

- - -

"Three Niner Alpha, this is Six-Six," said Ryan. "Sitrep, over."

"Three Niner Alpha. Send."

"Six-Six. We are holed up at grid"—he checked the GPS on his wrist—"Quebec Quebec 4133 8921. We have a section, section plus of insurgents encircling our location. We need QRF extraction, ASA-fucking-P. And we got some elder with crazy eyes who's just brought us inside his house. We'll strongpoint here. Over."

Around Ryan, the other snipers were staying low, out of sight of the windows and doorway. They had each dropped their rucks and were breaking down their gear. Magazines of bullets and grenades were being laid out on the carpets. Travis had unslung the Tac-50 and was extending the bipod. From outside the house, through the courtyard, came steady bursts of fire.

Meanwhile, the old man stood to the side of

one of the windows. He was watching the snipers prepare themselves with bemusement.

Ryan pressed his comms again. "Three Niner Alpha, this is Six-Six. Can you advise on that extraction, over?"

"Six-Six, this is Zero. Describe the friendly with the eyes."

That wasn't Jennifer's voice. That was the battle-group operations officer, Major Lavigne. It was good that higher was on the net—but asking about the old man's eyes?

"Zero, Six-Six," said Ryan. "Don't know if you heard my last but we need extraction now!"

A pause, then Lavigne's voice again: "Zero. I say again, describe the friendly. Over."

Ryan and Travis exchanged a quick, incredulous glance. Bleakly, Ryan thought, Thanks, higher headquarters—I ask you for help and you ask me how cute some old haji is.

"Six-Six," said Ryan. "The friendly is—I don't know, he's Afghan old. Maybe fifty. He's got a grey turban and man jams. His eyes are weird, different colours. One blue, one brown—"

Jennifer's voice briskly interrupted: "Break, break. Zero, they're jammed out there. Danger close for artillery and QRF is still twenty mikes away. We've gotta get them out."

Lavigne came back: "Three Niner Alpha, this Zero. Roger. We're pushing hard. Will advise. Out."

"Six-Six, this is Three Niner Alpha," said Jennifer. "Hunker down. We'll get you out of there ASAP."

"Six-Six, roger," said Ryan. "Out."

He thumbed off the comms. Then he put a fresh magazine into his C8.

"We're on our own, Warrant," said Tank. It wasn't a question.

"For a while," said Ryan.

Outside, the firing had stopped. But there were multiple voices shouting commands. In his mind's eye, Ryan could picture them: a dozen black-garbed Talibs taking support positions in the village square, forming up on either side of the compound doors . . . This brief break in the firing was only the calm before the storm.

Ryan was about to give direction when an inner door opened into the main room. Hickey snapped his weapon in the direction of the door, only to see the two little girls entering. Between them they were carrying a tarnished metal teapot and five glass mugs on a tray. The girls carefully set the tray at the elder's feet. One of them met Ryan's stare. She smiled shyly.

More shouting outside, then a heavy silence. The old man had his head cocked to the window. He crouched down and gently draped his arms around the little girls and whispered something to them. They nodded and exited the main room, going back through the inner door and closing it behind them.

"What in the actual fuck," said Hickey.

Two seconds more of that heavy silence.

"Okay," said Ryan. "Any second now. Tank, Trav, you're on the main door. Me and Hickey on the windows. Aimed shots. Try to make your rounds last. It's been a privilege, gents."

"Likewise," said Travis.

Ryan shouldered his C8 when the shuddering concussion came. The wooden doors in the compound wall—and a large section of the wall around the doors—were blown apart. Mud and straw and splintered wood and dust and smoke and sunlight poured through the gap. The insurgents must have used an RPG or a recoilless round. Each member of Six-Six tensed around his weapon, dripping sweat, waiting for the gunfire and the close-range charge to follow.

But then the old man cut across their line of sight. He moved through the courtyard almost at a stroll. Ryan hadn't even seen him leave the house. The old man was enveloped by the cloud hanging around the shattered doorway.

One second passed. Two seconds. The world would have been without sound were it not for the heartbeat pounding in Ryan's ears.

Five more seconds. Ten.

The dust in the breached wall was just starting to settle when the old man reappeared. He stopped in the middle of the courtyard, facing the house and the snipers inside it. His expression was composed, even serene. He gestured at the jagged hole.

"I think he's telling us we can go," Travis said softly.

Ryan waited a moment. The old man also waited, not moving. Ryan straightened up and let his C8 point at the ground. "Taliban?" he said.

At last the old man spoke. "No Taliban."

"We're safe to go?"

The old man nodded.

"Warrant," said Tank. "I don't know."

"What do you think?" said Travis.

"I think he means it," said Ryan. "If he wanted them to have us he could've let it happen before they blew his door down."

That much was openly true, but it was more than that. It was something Ryan couldn't articulate in his own thoughts, much less explain to his det. Ryan stepped out of the house and into the courtyard. He shifted his C8 to his left hand and put his right on his chest. He performed a shallow bow. "Salaam alaikum."

"Wa alaikum salaam," said the old man.

■ ■ ■

A few minutes later Six-Six had gathered up their weapons and ammunition and rehoisted their rucks. The old man watched them step off, sipping his tea. Six-Six made their way back into the village square. Empty shell casings twinkled in the dust, and the compound wall, on this side, was scored with bullet holes. But the square was devoid of people, villager and Taliban alike. Only the goat remained.

Ryan had already reported over his comms that the firefight was over. *Enemy has broken contact* was the only way he could explain it. Now he thumbed open the channel and said, "Three Niner Alpha, this is Six-Six. Sitrep. We're clearing the village, heading for Romeo-Victor at Quebec Quebec 4012 8883. Over."

"Three Niner Alpha, acknowledged," said Jennifer. "Rendezvous, Quebec Quebec 4012 8883."

The relief in her voice was unmistakable. Ryan couldn't blame her.

Before the det moved out of sight of the compound, Ryan looked back. But the old man with the different-coloured eyes was gone. Like a ghost, thought Ryan.

# 2

CAPTAIN PETE MITCHELL was in the battle group TOC on Kandahar Airfield when the report came up about the ambush that a Charlie Company sniper det—Six-Six, was it?—had sprung prematurely out on Hyena Road.

It was seven in the morning. Pete had gotten up at six, managed a half-hearted workout at the American gym, showered, put on his combats, and come over to the TOC to check in with the intelligence shop. He hadn't had breakfast yet and was hungry, although the thought of the flavourless scrambled eggs and overbrewed coffee in the multinational dining facility didn't do much for his appetite. Later that morning, he was scheduled to sit in on a meeting between the task force commander, Brigadier-General Rilmen, and a local power broker named Bashir Daoud Khan.

The subject of the meeting was Hyena Road. The subject of all Rilmen's meetings these days was Hyena Road. The road was the general's central project—the lasting mark he wanted to make on this country.

Rilmen wasn't the first foreign general to want to make a personal lasting mark on Afghanistan. Some variations of the country's history said that the name Kandahar was a derivative of Alexandria, one of many such places Alexander the Great had named for himself three centuries before Christ was born. With that pedigree in mind, Pete supposed General Rilmen could have his road. At least he hadn't named it for himself.

Pete checked in with the night-shift NCO in the little plywood-sided effects office. A quiet night, nothing significant to report. The NCO had probably watched pirated DVDs all night. Pete nodded, said he was going for breakfast and would be back in half an hour.

The NCO gave him an impassive shrug and yawned. "See you in a bit, sir."

Pete stepped out of the effects office into the central space of the TOC. Wood-framed desks lined the room, each stacked with computer terminals. Duty officers and NCOs were bent over the keyboards. The main sources of light in the TOC were the monitors and underneath the battle map in the middle of the room.

Pete stopped at a small coffee station in one corner. He held a Styrofoam cup under a dented metal urn and filled it up. This was the last of the overnight coffee, Pete was sure, but it was better than the crude oil in the DFAC. As he mixed some cream and sugar into the cup, he nodded to the operations officer, Rémi Lavigne, who'd come on shift twenty minutes ago. Lavigne nodded back.

Pete was about to make his way out of the TOC when one of the duty officers spoke up: "Troops in contact."

The already muted noise of the TOC went silent. "Where?" said Lavigne.

"In vicinity of Sperwan Ghar," said the duty officer. "Out along Hyena Road."

Pete stopped in his tracks.

"Put it on the speakers," said Lavigne.

One of the TOC signallers switched on the speakers. The transmissions from the Charlie Company command post, out at Sperwan Ghar, popped into the TOC for everyone to hear. Pete recognized the voice: Jenn Bowman, the acting company commander. Right now she was reporting that the company sniper det had sprung an ambush meant for a LAV convoy. Pete knew Jenn in passing. She was a competent, aggressive young woman—one of a handful of female infantry officers. Very easy on the eyes, as well.

Pete didn't need to stay in the TOC. This was Lavigne's fight to manage. But the mention of Hyena Road had captured Pete's attention. It seemed General Rilmen's own Alexandria had lit up yet again.

For the next little while, Pete stood by the battle map, listening without saying anything as Six-Six's contact went from bad to worse. The snipers were trying to exfiltrate south, cross-country, without being engaged on either side. Jenn Bowman was requesting fast air to support them, but there was nothing currently in range. On top of that, the battle group was getting reports from Kandahar City, where the local Afghan cops were dealing with a suicide bomber in a car who'd tried to blow up a police station. It was never one thing by itself around here. It was never simple.

"That's the third one this month," said Lavigne.

It took Pete a moment to realize the operations officer was talking to him. He blinked. "What's that, sir?"

"VBIED in the city, near a police station. Third one this month."

Pete nodded. There was a pattern there, a sign of something, but his mind was still locked on Hyena Road.

A short while later, Charlie Company's sniper det reported in from a village they'd holed up inside. Haji Baba. By this point, Lavigne had instructed the signallers to pipe the det's frequency into the TOC as well. Over the speakers, the master sniper's voice was heightened. He wasn't panicked, but the urgency of his situation was plain. In the background came sharp cracks of gunfire.

Pete looked at the battle map. One of the duty officers had plugged a pin down to indicate Haji Baba. The village was little more than a wide spot along an unnamed route three kilometres south of Hyena Road. Out there was proper enemy territory—seldom patrolled by friendly forces, rife with opium tracts and weapons caches.

This was a good time to slip out, Pete thought. He wasn't offering anything, and he had no desire to be listening in if the sniper det was overrun. He took a half-step away from the battle map.

Just then the master sniper's voice came on: "Six-Six. We are holed up at grid . . . Quebec Quebec 4133 8921. We have a section, section plus of insurgents encircling our location. We need QRF extraction, ASA-fucking-P. And we got some elder with crazy eyes who's just brought us inside his house. We'll strongpoint here. Over."

A strange feeling passed through Pete. He turned back around, trying not to spin on his heels. "Major Lavigne," he said. "Can you ask him about those crazy eyes?"

Lavigne frowned at Pete. Pete nodded. Lavigne picked up a headset and thumbed the switch. "Six-Six, this is Zero. Describe the friendly with the eyes."

A moment later the master sniper came back, sounding not just urgent but agitated. "Zero, Six-Six. Don't know if you heard my last but we need extraction now!"

Lavigne gave Pete a look that was both annoyed and expectant. Pete leaned across the battle map. "It's important. I need to know about those crazy eyes. Potential high-value indicator. It's important, Rémi."

Lavigne's eyes narrowed. But then he said, "Zero. I say again, describe the friendly. Over."

"Six-Six," said the sniper. "The friendly is—I don't know, he's Afghan old. Maybe fifty. He's got a grey turban and man jams. His eyes are weird, different colours. One blue, one brown—"

At that moment, Jenn Bowman's voice interrupted the exchange. A part of Pete was surprised it had taken her this long to intercede between the higher headquarters and the snipers in contact. "Break break. Zero, they're jammed out there. Danger close for artillery and QRF is still twenty mikes away. We've gotta get them out."

"Three Niner Alpha, this is Zero," said Lavigne. "Roger. We're pushing hard. Will advise. Out."

Lavigne put the headset down. The look he gave Pete was definitely annoyed. Pete lifted a hand to signify that he didn't need anything more for the moment.

Pete did not end up going to breakfast in the DFAC. He got himself a cold Pop-Tart from the coffee station and stayed in the TOC throughout the rest of the incident. He listened as the snipers reported the strabge end to the event, Enemy has broken contact, and he listened to their replorts of exfiltration. Six-Six's RV with the LAVs, some thirty minutes later, occurred without incident, and half an hour after that they were back in Sperwan Ghar. No friendly casualties. The sense of relief in the battle group TOC was palpable.

Pete, on the other hand, was distracted. He had to get ready for his meeting with Rilmen, and to do that he had to turn his thoughts back to Hyena Road, but . . .

One eye blue, one eye brown.

Couldn't be, he thought.

= = =

"I've built a road, gentlemen," said General Rilmen. "A big fucking road and it's like a dagger driving straight into the heart of the enemy and it is fucking him up. Every morning he wakes up, I'm standing there and I'm punching him in the fucking face."

The commander's briefing room in the task

force headquarters was a bit better appointed than the vast majority of the other facilities around KAF. The plywood walls had a pale finish and were mounted with large flat-screen televisions; the long meeting table was covered by a patterned cloth; wide windows overlooked the headquarters compound and the solemn memorial monument outside. An Afghan flag and a Canadian flag, both furled, stood in the corners at the head of the room. A number of framed photographs hung on the wall. The photographs showed various successes and milestones—a school opening, a hospital being built, a new well in a village somewhere, a small group of local children receiving vaccinations. These were all the achievements of past commanders, Rilmen's predecessors; as of yet, there was no photograph of Hyena Road. It was late fall of the preceding year when the construction of the road had begun, following a huge set of orders with Rilmen's signature on them. Before Hyena there had been just a dirt track running west from Sperwan Ghar down into the southernmost tip of Panjwayi, where the Taliban still openly held the terrain. The first phase of the road's construction consisted of Operation Jackal, which was an aggressive ISAF-led clearance mission through the district. Op Jackal went through the sullen Kandahari winter; walls were levelled, homes were destroyed, hundreds of thousands of American dollars were paid out in compensation, and more than sixty insurgents were killed in the process.

Just after New Year's Day, roadwork began. Platoons of combat engineers, Canadian and American alike, worked alongside four hundred local contractors and labourers. The pitch to the locals was that ISAF money and steady work was better than throwing in with the bad guys. Not that the construction was easy going; starting almost immediately, there were hit-and-run attacks on the workers every day and IEDs laid down for the gravel trucks. The hulls of destroyed trucks were usually just dumped by the side of the road, nothing else to be done for them. Many of the trucks were still there even now, eerie testaments to the blood that had been spilled throughout Hyena's construction.

But Rilmen was relentless. He would have his road. And by the end of May it was almost finished, all eighteen kilometres of it, Sperwan Ghar down to Mushan.

Around the meeting table, comfortable faux-leather chairs provided seating for a handful of senior staff and visitors—the task force sergeant major, the legal advisor, two American full-bird colonels, and four Canadian lieutenant-colonels, including Lieutenant-Colonel Armstrong, the task force's chief intelligence officer. Pete's boss. The remainder of the attendees, mainly staff officers with serious expressions on their faces, were all standing in a tight knot at the back of the room. This number included Pete. Beside him was Chewey, Lieutenant Cheryl Jeffries. She was short, round, and cute. Pete was quite fond of her.

Brigadier-General Daniel Rilmen was also standing, at the front of the room next to an enormous map of Kandahar Province. Rilmen was a big man. He had huge hands, and his head, set between his linebacker shoulders, was shaved bald. He was almost too big to be real, it seemed—more of a caricature than a man. Sometimes Rilmen made Pete think of Lex Luthor from the Superman comics. Other times Rilmen reminded Pete of Marlon Brando playing Kurtz in *Apocalypse Now.*

At the meeting this morning, Rilmen's vibe

was Lex Luthor: dynamic, ambitious—and potentially capable of conducting shady business if it meant getting his way. That shady business had a name and a face and was slouched in one of the comfortable chairs around the table. Bashir Daoud Khan, chairman of the provincial council, was in his late forties. He wore a pinstripe blazer over tailored shalwar kameez, and on his head was a peaked woollen *karakul*. Khan's beard, black shot through with silver, was neatly manicured. He had one elbow on the table and his chin propped on his fist. He was smiling blandly. The smile did not touch his eyes.

Beside Khan was his son, Hamid, dressed almost identically to his father but with an embroidered *kufi* instead of a *karakul*. Underneath the *kufi*, Hamid's hair was a thick black slick, parted to one side. He was seventeen or eighteen and clean-shaven, and he was almost permanently grinning. As far as Pete could tell from the dozen or so times he'd seen the kid in person, Hamid Khan's perpetual grin was meant to show off the garish ruby-and-gold-studded braces across his front teeth.

At the front of the room, Rilmen tapped one

sausage-like middle finger—it *had* to be the middle finger—against the map of the province. "We've never been this deep into the Horn of Panjwayi before, but Hyena Road is in there now. How many kilometres, Shorty?"

The task force sergeant major, Shorty Hastings, so-named because he didn't stand an inch over five feet, said, "Eighteen, sir."

"Eighteen," said Rilmen. "Eighteen kilometres, there to stay, gentlemen. The Taliban doesn't like it, 'cause it's fucking with their freedom of movement. So they're going after the dump trucks and the gravel trucks and the workers—"

The elder Khan seemed to perk up. One heavy eyebrow lifted. In English, he said, "General, are you saying—"

"I'm saying I've had thirty-six civilians killed in the last four months and this shit's gotta stop," said Rilmen. The general crossed his arms. "I need *your* help."

Khan spread his hands wide. It was a slow, grand gesture. "I am just one man."

"With his own militia," said Rilmen.

Khan dipped his chin in a shallow nod, as if to say, *You got me there.* That bland smile pulled at the corners of his mouth again. Pete mentally went through a checklist of Khan's assets and holdings: the private militia, formally described as a personal security force, which consisted of a few dozen local hard cases; the businesses in Kandahar City, which included two car dealerships, four autobody shops, and a handful of restaurants; the shares in almost countless wheat and grape farms outside the city; and, of course, the seat on the council. That was the official inventory on Khan. The unofficial tally ran the gamut from opium to guns to child brides bound for Dubai. Nothing could be said publicly, of course, because Khan was an ally . . .

As if on cue, Khan said, "I am your partner in peace, General Rilmen. Now and forever."

Rilmen's face remained composed. So did the faces of the other senior advisors around the table. Without doubt, everyone knew what Pete knew about Khan. It was an open secret. *Partner in peace* indeed.

"So," said Rilmen. "Hyena Road will formally open in two weeks. We'll make an event of it, naturally. The power of symbolism cannot be underestimated. Until the road opens, I'll continue to need your eyes and your ears. And when the time comes, at the dedication ceremony, I need your presence, Mr. Khan. You and your son. The public face of partnership."

"Of course, General," said Khan.

Rilmen planted his fists on the meeting table and leaned forward. "Your presence at the dedication ceremony would send a very strong message—to your countrymen and the insurgents both."

A shadow of discomfort, gone as soon as it appeared, passed over Khan's face. Maybe he had an upset stomach. He turned to his son and nodded.

Hamid Khan stood up. The young man cleared his throat and launched into a declaration, in English, that had obviously been rehearsed: "Hyena Road is a gift for all Afghans. My father and I would be honoured to attend your ceremony."

Rilmen, still leaning forward, made a fist with his right hand and slugged the tabletop. His RMC ring made a noise like a pistol shot. "Outstanding," said the general.

- - -

A few minutes later, the meeting was breaking up. The senior staff were all standing, taking turns shaking hands with Khan. From across the room, Pete watched as Hamid Khan chatted like an old pal with Shorty and one of the American colonels. The American said something. Shorty laughed. Hamid Khan grinned. The gold and rubies on his front teeth glittered in the midmorning light through the window.

Chewey hung close to Pete. "Look at those pricks," she said. "Father and son. It'd be a fuck of a lot easier to do what we came here to do if the both of them stopped breathing for some reason."

"I hear you," said Pete.

"We've got intel about the son," said Chewey. "Apparently he's become his old man's main payment collector in the city. He goes around with three bodyguards, making all the junkies pay up. And he's not even twenty years old."

"The trouble with Bashir Khan is he's so well connected," said Pete. "There's a gigantic house of cards built around him. He's got us, he's got the CIA, the Pakistanis, you name it. Buddy knows how to play his advantages. You take someone like him out, you don't know who's gonna fill the vacuum."

"So what's the best way to deal with a guy like that?"

"You neutralize him somehow," said Pete. "You find another player, someone who can cancel him out . . ." Pete trailed off. Something was tickling the back of his mind.

"Earth to Pete," said Chewey.

He shook his head. Whatever that tickle was, it was gone now. "Hey," he said. "Did you hear about that TIC on Hyena this morning?"

She nodded. "I did. And it looks like the boss is getting the good news right now."

Pete looked over. One of the studious-looking staff officers was speaking quietly to General Rilmen. Pete couldn't make out what was being said, but the staff officer was pointing to the map—to the very point on Hyena Road where the sniper det had sprung the ambush. Rilmen's brow was furrowed and deep colour was flooding into his face. Pete watched as the staff officer tapped the map again. A short distance below the officer's fingertip was a small dark marking.

The village, Haji Baba.

Pete looked from the map to the senior Khan, a metre away from Rilmen. Khan, smiling a used-car salesman's smile, was in close conversation with Lieutenant-Colonel Armstrong. The sounds of the room seemed to blur into a dull roar.

Chewey poked Pete's ribs. "Hey, there you go again."

Pete blinked. "I'm here," he said. "Just thinking about something. Did you ever hear about Alexander the Great's dirt story?" Pete could tell by the look on Chewey's face that she had not. He went on, "Well, Alexander the Great marched into this graveyard twenty-five hundred years ago. Easy to march in, hard to march out. Those were his words. He and his mother wrote to each other all the time. And one day he got a letter from her saying, What the fuck? You conquered most of the known world in, like, a day and a half—what are you doing bogged down in Afghanistan? He grabbed a bag and shovelled it full of dirt and had it sent back to Greece with a message to his mother: Take this dirt and dump it around the palace. See what happens. So Alexander's mother spread the dirt all around the palace. Later that night a couple of attendants showed up, to make sure she was all right. One says, 'Go ahead, after you.' And the other says, 'No, after you.' And the first one says, 'No, I insist.' And the second one says, 'Don't you fucking tell me what to do,' and they both pull their swords and go at it until they kill each other. Alexander's mother watched all this and wrote him a letter saying, Okay, okay, now I get it. And he wrote back, saying, Yeah, even the dirt is hostile."

Chewey's eyebrows lifted. "Is there a moral to this story, professor?"

"Yeah. In Afghanistan, dogs fight dogs, birds fight birds, men kill men. Tell Armstrong I'll come see him after lunch."

"You could hang with me," said Chewey.

"I could," said Pete. "But the future of Western civilization depends on my ass getting out to Sperwan Ghar."

= = =

At sixteen-thirty that afternoon, a Chinook helicopter lifted off from one of the chopper pads at KAF. The vast, ugly industrial sprawl of the airbase fell away below as the big double-rotor bird climbed into the sky. Two Griffons stayed close to the Chinook's airspace, providing escort and observation for ground-based threats. A dozen Canadian soldiers—a mixed bunch, some coming back from leave, some returning from the KAF infirmary, two or three on various liaison tasks, one special forces operator on God-knew-what kind of business—were crammed into the sling seats. There was scarcely enough room for the soldiers themselves, let alone their weapons and kit. A young male journalist, newly arrived in-country, looked around with wide eyes. The journalist's body was soft and fat, bulging around his body armour. A pale-blue helmet sat crookedly on his head. The Chinook's final passenger was Pete.

After the meeting in Rilmen's briefing room, Pete had gone straight back to Rémi Lavigne in the battle group TOC. He made his pitch to Lavigne over a coffee. Lavigne didn't seem to care one way or the other; even Pete's second use of the term *high value indicator* didn't carry much interest with the operations officer. However, as it turned out, Pete was in luck. A troop-lift flight was bound for Sper that very afternoon, and the following morning, a patrol was scheduled to head out to the village. The purpose of the patrol would be twofold: assess damage compensation and give a journalist from Montreal an opportunity to see the work of Canadian troops up close. Pete could tag along, said Lavigne with a shrug, if Pete's boss didn't have an issue with it.

Normally Lieutenant-Colonel Armstrong would've been a harder sell. Armstrong was notoriously cautious about letting the officers in his shop go out on patrols. *We're mainly advisors*, Armstrong would say. *We don't need to get out on the pointy end, where we can't see the forest for the trees. That's the grunts' job.* But Armstrong was less than two weeks away from going on leave—he'd signed up for some kind of over-forty singles' tour in Tahiti—and his attention was galvanized on that. When Pete went to see him after lunch, Armstrong gave some distracted pushback.

"Well, I just don't know, Captain Mitchell. Sperwan Ghar is out on the pointy end."

"If I'm right, sir, this could impact the Hyena Road dedication ceremony," said Pete. "Which in turn could screw your leave."

That was all he needed. Ninety minutes later

Pete was stuffing himself into the Chinook along with the journalist and the other passengers. Pete had his shaving stuff and a change of underwear and some notebooks jammed into a patrol pack. His rifle was propped between his knees, butt-down on the floor panelling.

High value indicator, thought Pete. Crazy eyes. One blue, one brown. He thought also of Bashir Daoud Khan. Hamid Khan and his ridiculous braces.

At that moment, the big chopper lurched in the air, banking stiffly to the right. Pete's stomach did a sick loop-the-loop. He gripped his rifle tightly, hoping they weren't in the midst of some kind of evasive manoeuvre against fire coming from the ground. The Chinook was a nice target for a surface-to-air missile. Pete felt almost as uncomfortable as the journalist looked; it had been well over a month since the last time he'd gone outside the wire. Beside Pete, two of the other soldiers cursed loudly. They were barely audible over the engine noise and the din of the rotors. The special forces guy was sleeping.

---

Whatever the steep banking had been about, the troop-lift flight made it in one piece to the landing zone at Sperwan Ghar. The Griffons stayed in the air; the Chinook touched down, ochre-coloured dust spiralling up around it, and stayed only as long as it took to let its passengers debark. No pilots liked to hover in the airspace around here, drawing the interest of concealed eyes and weapons in the surrounding grape fields. Within a few minutes, the Chinook lifted skyward again and zipped away in the direction of KAF.

The other passengers dispersed almost immediately. A couple of soldiers came and met the journalist and escorted him away. Pete momentarily stood on the LZ, taking in his surroundings. He'd never been to Sper before, but it looked almost exactly the same as every other friendly outpost throughout the province. The same gravel ground, the same Hesco bastion walls, the same concrete blast barriers, the same spools of concertina wire, the same antenna farm, the same dust-laden tents, the same squat watchtowers along the perimeter. The Ghar itself was a rocky pimple jutting up from the naked earth. At the summit of the Ghar, Pete could just make out the profile of an observation post; up there would be a commanding view in all directions. Hold the high ground, thought Pete. A central tenet of warfare since . . . well, since long before even Alexander tried to conquer this land.

He checked in first at the company CP, hoping he might find Jenn Bowman. The CP, a vastly scaled-down version of the battle group TOC, was located inside a pre-existing mud-walled blockhouse that had been repurposed for the task. Jenn wasn't there. The sergeant on duty said she was working out, then having supper, and would be back at eighteen hundred. Pete asked if anyone knew he'd be coming, if the message about his visit had made it down from battle group yet. The duty sergeant just shrugged. Visitors came and went with a fair amount of regularity around here; nobody really cared about some stray captain—as long as he stayed out of the way—coming in from KAF to tag onto a patrol.

Pete dropped his pack and vest on a cot in one of the transient tents, then slung his rifle over his shoulder and made his way over to the mess tent. It was seventeen-forty now and the sun was in the west. Pete cleaned up at the hand-wash station.

He got a paper plate and a set of plastic utensils and fell in line. Dinner was roast beef with string beans. The meat looked tough and overdone, but Pete had found that the food at the outposts was always better than what came out of the huge industrial kitchens back on KAF.

He emerged from the mess tent, carrying his plate in one hand and a bottle of water in the other. Here was a small common area. There were crooked picnic tables, a tiny basketball court, a makeshift ball-hockey rink where a small group of soldiers in PT clothing was playing a loud pickup game. Pete was about to sit down by himself when, at last, he spotted Jenn Bowman. She was on the other side of the common area, sitting in a collapsible camp chair. Beside her was a lean, dark-haired soldier Pete didn't recognize, also relaxing in a camp chair.

As Pete got close to the two chairs, he noticed Jenn Bowman's hand. It was dangling down beside her chair, very close to the hand of the man beside her. Touching, almost. She looked up when Pete had closed the distance to a metre, and drew her dangling hand into her lap. It was a quick, unconscious gesture. Pete was amused. The soldier beside Jenn—a warrant officer by the rank slip-on on his chest—remained unreadable.

"Jennifer," said Pete. "Sorry to interrupt. I just got here."

She squinted at him. "Pete, hi. Welcome to Sper."

"You knew I was coming, right?"

"Major Lavigne dropped me a line a couple of hours ago," said Jennifer. "I got the general gist of it, but can you give me some specifics?"

The warrant officer still hadn't said anything. He'd laced his fingers together over his midsection. If he was irked that Pete had interrupted whatever moment he was having with Jennifer, he gave no indication of it.

"I'll bring you up to speed, Jenn," said Pete. "But before that, I was wondering if I could have a word with the master sniper who was in that TIC this morning. Can you introduce me?"

Jennifer and the warrant officer shared a brief glance. Jennifer looked as if she were about to say something but appeared to stop herself. She seemed to think for a few seconds. And then, smiling, she said, "Captain Mitchell, meet Warrant Officer Ryan Murphy, call sign Six-Six."

Jennifer told them she had to get back to the CP. She took her empty plate and a crushed juice box and stood up and walked away. Pete sat down in the chair she'd vacated. He propped his supper on his knee and tried to cut into it with his plastic knife. The sniper, Warrant Murphy, was watching Jenn go.

"I might be out of line," said Pete. "But on behalf of the entire battle group I'd like to express our collective jealousy."

The sniper shot Pete a sharp, narrow-eyed look.

Pete laughed. "I don't care, Warrant . . . Ryan, was it? It's no business of mine. You two might want to be a little more subtle, but otherwise fill your boots."

Ryan seemed to relax a little. A small smile creased his lips. "Are you married, Captain?"

"Call me Pete. And yes, I am. She's the woman of my dreams."

"Does she know what you do?"

"She's been through the drill before," said Pete. "This is my third tour. But she thinks I work inside the wire. Which is true, most of the time. I don't see any reason to dispel that notion. Let her sleep easy at night."

"Considerate," said Ryan.

Pete chewed a mouthful of the tough beef. He chased it with water. When he'd swallowed, he said, "I was in the TOC this morning during your TIC in Haji Baba. You guys were lucky."

"You came all the way out here to tell me that?"

"No. Listen. How much do you know about Pashtunwali?"

Ryan gave him another look, this one measuring. "The tribal code? I know what's in the handbook, I guess. It's old."

Pete nodded. "Pashtunwali *is* old. So old they think of Islam as a kind of recent add-on to it. Anyway, the code's got a bunch of what they call pillars, and one of them is *panah*. It means 'protection,' more or less. When that elder invited you into his home? That was *panah*. No harm could come to you."

"So, what, I owe him now?"

"He did it for Allah, not for you," said Pete. "But you and your boys did make it out. No injuries, right?"

Ryan shook his head. "Couple bumps and bruises, but yeah, no, no injuries."

Neither man needed to say what an unlikely miracle that had been. A few quiet moments passed, time enough for Pete to finish his supper. He folded the plastic cutlery into the paper plate and put them down onto the gravel beside them. Then he took a pack of smokes out of the sleeve pocket of his combats. He took a cigarette out for himself and offered the pack to Ryan. Ryan shook his head no.

"Did the elder speak any English?" said Pete, lighting up.

"A couple words. *No Taliban*. That's about all."

"Were there any marks on him? Scars?"

"Not that I recall, but he did have a limp. His right leg. Not much of one either—not like he'd been crippled from birth or anything like that."

"Anything else?"

"Yeah," said Ryan. "He had different eyes. One was brown. The other was blue. Really blue."

Pete blew out a long stream of smoke. "Indeed. The crazy eyes. You remember getting pestered about that over the net this morning?"

"Yes I do," said Ryan. "Middle of a gunfight, higher's asking me what this old local looks like."

Pete chuckled. "My fault."

"Right," said Ryan. "So, then, who is this guy? And why'd he give us his protection?"

"A really goddamn good question," said Pete. "There's a patrol going out to Haji Baba tomorrow morning, oh nine hundred. Some CIMIC stuff—looking at battle damage to the village— and a little show-and-tell for a journalist. I'm going as well, but my role is, well, on the downlow for now. Could you tag along? Maybe ID the elder for me?"

A long moment. Pete thought Ryan might say no, but finally the sniper shrugged. "If I can clear it with the CP I'll be there."

"Inshallah," said Pete, smiling.

# 3

THIS TIME OF YEAR, sundown over Kandahar Province was long and slow. The ever-present
dust in the air gave a reddish hue to the day's
last light. Out at Sperwan Ghar, sundown always
had a simmering tension; the gathering dark was
often punctuated by harassing small-arms fire
or the odd rocket or mortar attack. The harass-
ment was ineffective most of the time, but it kept
everyone on edge.

This evening had stayed quiet. So far. Ryan,
wearing a T-shirt and a towel around his hips and
flip-flops on his feet, was going into the shower
trailer. He thought about a Chinese-made rocket
shrieking down from the sky and taking him
out. He thought about dying in his T-shirt and
flip-flops and nothing else. The image made him
chuckle dryly. The bright interior of the trailer

was the same as always: foggy with steam, mud on the floors, other men crammed between the showers and the sinks. Raucous jokes were being traded back and forth. Someone was singing off-key. Ryan shouldered his way through the crowd, nodding to a few guys he knew. He wished he'd come later, twenty-one or twenty-two hundred, when the crowd in the trailer usually thinned out at least by half. On the other hand, he was tired—hollowed out from the events of the day, the morning especially—and wanted nothing more than to turn in.

He waited until one of the shower stalls was vacated. He slipped off his T-shirt and towel, stepped into the stall, and pulled the water-stained plastic curtain closed behind him. The water pouring over his head was hot only for a moment, then it turned tepid. Before long it would be cold as ice. He didn't care. This was his second shower since they'd come back from the clusterfuck at Haji Baba. He still felt oddly unwashed. It was a mental thing, he knew, and it didn't make any sense. But he also knew he wouldn't be able to fall asleep without smelling the soap on his skin.

As he scrubbed his arms and chest, his mind

wandered back. It wasn't Haji Baba or Hyena Road or the morning's TIC he was revisiting—instead it was the conversation he'd had with Jenn before that weird first-name-basis effects captain had interrupted them.

They'd been sitting in the camp chairs, Jenn and Ryan, each having a paper plateful of supper. For a while they'd stayed quiet, watching the shinny game on the makeshift rink, just enjoying each other's company. After a while, she'd said, "What are you thinking, Warrant Murphy?"

"Oh, nothing good," said Ryan. "Maybe our hotel room in Cyprus. Maybe that certain thing you like to do."

She smiled—was it a little bit sad?—and turned her face away to look at something. "That's a pretty good thought. And I do like to do that thing. Very much."

"You're pretty good at it," said Ryan.

Before he could say anything else, she looked right at him, and her expression was sad. He felt something catch in the pit of his stomach. "I gotta say something here," said Jenn. "It's going to be shitty but it has to be said." Before Ryan could reply, she went on: "I am completely crazy about you. As you know. And Cyprus was . . . perfect. We're perfect. But we can't keep doing this. We both know that."

Countless possible responses went through Ryan's mind, but he only said one word. "Fuck."

"The fraternization thing is bad enough," she said. "Never mind the officer—NCO part. And never mind the fact that I thought I was gonna lose my mind today, when you were out there and I was in the CP, and anything could've . . . If we get caught, I'll be cashiered. This is my career—"

"It's mine, too."

"I know it is. I know. Look. When we rotate home, we'll see. But right now, while we're here? It's got to stop."

"So this is it?" said Ryan.

She looked away again. "I think it has to be."

"This is like fucking Armageddon," Ryan muttered. In his mind, the phrase had sounded dramatic and profound. But out loud it sounded kind of silly. It was like when he'd said *emanating* over the radio and she'd said it back to him, her amusement coming through loud and clear.

"I know," said Jenn. "And *you* should know there's nothing I'd rather do right now than climb all over you and fraternize the shit out of you."

"Hey, Captain Bowman. You can't dump me in one sentence and talk like that in the next. It's inhuman."

She gave him that sad smile again. Their hands were both dangling beside their camp chairs. Close together. Close enough for the fingers to brush—and that was when the intelligence captain strolled over to make his presence known and ask his questions.

Ryan finished his shower—the water had turned frigid—and opened the curtain. He stepped out and towelled off. Then he made his way to one of the sinks and rubbed the steam off the steel mirror. He brought out his shaving cream and razor and set to work. Maybe that captain (*Call me Pete*) had come at a good time. Maybe he'd saved Ryan from saying anything too fucking dumb.

And, Ryan thought as he tapped his razor against the side of the sink, what Pete had talked about *was* intriguing. That much was true. It was funny, because Pete really hadn't given away much at all. He'd talked around some things. He'd talked around the elder with the crazy eyes.

The roundabout talk was enough to set the hook, Ryan realized. And so, when Pete had asked him if he'd tag along, back out to Haji Baba where Ryan and his snipers had very nearly had their clocks punched—*that very fucking morning, no less*—Ryan's answer was yes. Yes, because the hook was set. He wanted to know more.

If there was one thing that could pull his thoughts away from Jenn, Ryan supposed, from what had seemed to be their breakup, it was the crazy-eyed elder.

- - -

Later that evening, Ryan was lying on his cot in his bunkspace inside Six-Six's mod tent. Each sniper had his own space, about three metres by three metres, partitioned off from the rest of the tent by thin canvas walls. Ryan couldn't hear much over the perpetual grind of the air conditioner. The only other guy in the tent was Hickey, earbuds in, playing a game or watching porn on his laptop. Ryan had seen him when he'd come in from the showers. Tank was lifting weights in what passed for the Sperwan Ghar gym, and

Travis was in one of the morale trailers, Skyping with his wife.

The events of that morning had been harrowing. There was no question about it. But as Ryan knew, each of his snipers compartmentalized it, stowed it away privately. Each sniper would be ready to step off on the next mission. The real time to deal with their own heads would come later, much later, on leave or decompression. Or back home, post-tour. That was the way it was. In the meantime, all Ryan could do was keep his eyes on his guys, watch to see if any of them were coming apart. He doubted that any of them would.

He tried to read for a little while, some paperback sci-fi story he'd pulled out of the free book bin at Canada House, his last time at KAF. His thoughts naturally wandered back to Jenn. Jenn and the elder. Before long his eyes started to get heavy, in spite of the things on his mind. He'd never had any trouble falling asleep when the time to rack out came, and for that he was very grateful.

He set the sci-fi novel down and was just about asleep when something occurred to him, woke him back up. Some further setting of the hook.

He would get sleepy again soon enough, but first he needed to see what he could find out. It was something Pete had talked about.

Ryan sat up, swung his legs onto the floor. He pulled one of his barrack boxes out from beneath his cot. The box was full of papers and books and binders. Most of them were weapons manuals and *aides-mémoire*. He sorted through them, vaguely wondering how the Afghan dust could get inside a box he hadn't opened in months.

Almost at the bottom of the box, he found what he was looking for: the Afghan cultural primer for ISAF troops. His copy had been darkly stained with coffee at some point. He didn't remember when. He laid back on his cot and opened the manual to the index at the back. The P section. *Pashtunwali*.

He flipped to the corresponding page. There were only a hundred words on the topic. Pashtunwali was ancient, as he knew, predating Islam; Pashtunwali dominated Pashtun life, especially outside the cities, even to this day; Pashtunwali stood on a small number of central tenets or pillars. Ryan's eyes roved over these. There was *panah*, also called *melmastia*, as Pete had said.

It was a concept of both hospitality and protection, no matter who was seeking it. There was *nang*, which meant honour, the saving of face. There was *tureh*, bravery, and *sabat*, loyalty. And lastly, as Ryan's eyes started to get heavy, there was *badal*. Revenge for a wrongdoing. Revenge that might take the form of violence lasting generations.

In his final moment before sleep, Ryan's thoughts were not of Jenn, or Pete, or the man they'd shot on the road that morning, or the crazy-eyed old man who'd given them sanctuary. His thoughts were of *badal*. Blood feuds lasting decades or longer. That was the truth of this place.

· · ·

At zero eight forty-five the next morning, the foot patrol from Sperwan Ghar was assembled near the strongpoint's front entrance. The central element of the patrol was a Canadian CIMIC detachment under the command of a sergeant named Osborne. The det was going to Haji Baba to assess the battle damage—and appropriate compensation—from the shootout the day before.

Also attached was an American K-9 sergeant with a bomb-sniffing German shepherd on a leash. The dog was sitting patiently, pink tongue lolling out of its mouth. A small squad of soldiers from the Afghan National Army were partnered with the patrol; these men, all of them improbably thin and short, were dressed in ill-fitting fatigues and oversized helmets. The tiniest among them, little more than a boy, had an RPG balanced like a yoke over his shoulders and a satchel full of warheads slung from his back. The journalist who'd arrived on the Chinook was present, more wide-eyed than ever. And lastly were Pete and Ryan, sticking to the edge of the group.

The Canadian soldiers were mostly smoking and joking and drinking from Styrofoam cups of coffee while the CIMIC det second-in-command fiddled around with his radio. Ryan had gone into the CP—nominally to advise the duty staff that he was departing with the patrol to Haji Baba—after he'd had breakfast. Jenn wasn't there. Ryan had hung around, pretending to look at the maps and the radio logs. It had taken him a few minutes to realize he didn't know what he was doing or why he was hanging around—he had no idea what he would say to her beyond the formal exchange between an NCO and an officer. For the time being, what other way could it be? What she'd said the night before came back to him: *When we rotate home, we'll see. But right now, while we're here? It's got to stop.* So he'd left the CP before she'd appeared, pushing his feelings away, to go and listen in on the last few minutes of Sergeant Osborne's patrol orders to his CIMIC det.

Now, as Ryan stood near Sper's front entrance, all he wanted was to get going. Overhead the sky was cloudless and the morning sun was searing. As far as the weather went, this day was indistinguishable from the days that had preceded it, going back two or three months. There hadn't been a drop of rain. Ryan adjusted his MBITR headset and shifted his body armour and tightened the sling on his C8. The last few moments before a patrol—any patrol— were always the worst. Hurry up and wait, as the old saying went.

A few paces away, the wide-eyed journalist was receiving some final instructions from Sergeant Osborne. The journalist was wearing a backpack full of gear, and around his neck was a Canon camera with an enormous telephoto lens.

"Remember, if you see wire or metal or plastic or newly turned dirt, don't step on it," said Osborne. "If you didn't drop it, don't pick it up. Try and keep five body lengths between you and the next man in the patrol. Inside the village you're going to see women in bags—you know, niqabs or what-have-you. Please don't look at them. I know you've probably seen that kind of outfit in Toronto or wherever you call home, but you haven't seen it here. If you stare at them here it can really fuck things up for us. Roger so far?"

The journalist could only nod.

Osborne patted down some of the items attached to the journalist's body armour. "This is your QuikClot. This here is a field dressing. Here's a tourniquet—"

The journalist made a guilty face. "I—I don't know how to use any of this stuff, to be honest."

Osborne grinned and clapped the journalist on the arm. "Sir, if any of this stuff needs to be used, it won't be you using it."

There was a pause, and then the journalist's face went white as he realized what Osborne was telling him. Ryan couldn't help but smile a little.

Just then, Pete Mitchell sidled up beside him. Pete looked a little stiff and out-of-practice in his body armour—he'd already sweated through his combats in a few places—but he wasn't the most fucked-up tag-along Ryan had ever seen. Pete was carrying a C7 with a fresh sheen of oil creeping out of the seam between the upper and lower receivers. He seemed to know what Ryan was thinking, because he grinned sheepishly and said, "I'm an intel officer. I don't get out much."

Before Ryan could reply, his headset crackled. It was the CIMIC det second-in-command, radio-checking with the CP: "Three Niner Alpha, this is Three Two Charlie, stepping off now, over."

The voice that came back was Jennifer's. She was in the CP now. "Three Niner Alpha, acknowledged."

A complicated emotion passed through Ryan's stomach. He suppressed it hard and fast.

"We're good to go, Sarge," the det second-in-command called to Sergeant Osborne.

Osborne nodded and made his way to the

front of the group. "All right, weapons ready and on safe everywhere. Fall in, game on."

---

As soon they'd left Sperwan Ghar, the CIMIC patrol and its various guests cut south, cross-country, toward Haji Baba. The total distance to the village was not more than six kilometres, but it was slow going over the grape fields and rocks and ancient, broken walls. They were walking, not driving, so that they could get an updated view of that part of the countryside, which hadn't been closely patrolled in about a month. The patrol moved in a long single file, halting regularly, each soldier taking a knee and scanning his arcs. The American dog handler stayed up front so that the dog could lead them with its nose. The journalist, directly in front of Ryan, looked like he was getting into the swing of things; although he was dripping with sweat, he was taking picture after picture, mostly of the Afghan soldiers partnered with the Canadians.

Halfway to Haji Baba, the patrol did a long halt while the dog sniffed at a particular pile of pebbles. The soldiers moved into an all-around defence. Ryan positioned himself on the north part of the formation. In the hazy distance he could make out the top of the rocky high feature he and his snipers had shot their way down from yesterday. The crags looked utterly unchanged, unremarkable. Why should there be anything different? Those old rocks didn't care who lived or died on them.

To Ryan's left, Pete was taking advantage of the long halt to slip his boot off and shake a stone out of it. Ryan took a draw of water from his CamelBak and watched Pete. *When that elder invited you into his home*, Pete had said, *that was* panah. *No harm could come to you.*

It baffled Ryan. All the events of yesterday morning, now more than ever. He found he wanted to see the old man again. He wanted to hear whatever it was Pete had to ask him. He wanted to understand. And yet he had a strange feeling that the old man wasn't going to be there today.

A minute or two later, the pebbles turned out to be nothing. Perhaps there was old explosive residue around there and that was what had attracted the dog. In any case, the patrol was shortly on the move again. Pete hastily finished tying up his boot. He got to his feet. Ryan adjusted his C8 and fell into step.

The distance to Haji Baba got less and less. Before long a solitary grape-drying hut came into view. As the patrol passed the hut, the wall around the village was visible in the near distance. A small number of farmers were working in the surrounding fields. That kind of thing was called *normal pattern of life* and it was a good indication. When the fields were empty, when the village was shuttered, that's when you really needed to worry. Yesterday . . . yesterday had been like that. No pattern of life.

Within the next ten minutes, the patrol had entered Haji Baba proper. The American dog-handler kept himself and his shepherd at the edge of the village; Afghans didn't like dogs in general and were usually terrified of the big breeds. There was no sense damaging any goodwill when it wasn't necessary.

Inside the village, the various buildings were still riddled with bullet holes, but the little central square was alive and vibrant. The shops were all open, men in dusty robes were hawking produce and arguing with each other, a number of animals—chickens and goats and sheep—were milling around, and everywhere there were children. The kids were dressed in an odd assortment of clothes, all as bright and innocent-looking as they were dirty and scruffy. A little boy, no older than five, ran up to Ryan and presented his hand for a high-five. Ryan remembered the two young girls he'd seen in the old man's compound. He looked around the square but he could not pick them out.

On the other side of the square, the gaping hole remained in the compound's outer wall. Ryan could see the main building beyond. He could see the very doorway he'd crouched in, waiting to make a last stand. Now, as yesterday, the doorway was almost black in contrast to the bright daylight; nothing could be seen of the interior of the building.

Not far away, two women in blue burqas scurried by on a lane off the square. It was the same lane Ryan and his snipers had come down yesterday. The journalist gaped at the robed figures.

"Hey!" Sergeant Osborne called. "Eyes front, sir!"

---

Ryan's instinct was right. The old man was nowhere to be seen.

A short while after arriving in Haji Baba, Osborne, Pete, Ryan, and one of the Afghan soldiers—an interpreter named Walid—were invited to a *shura* with some of the local men. The *shura* was held inside one of the buildings fronting the square, but not Ryan's Alamo compound. The inside of this new building was almost the same: carpets on the dirt floor, lamps on the bare walls, not a stick of furniture. A boy came into the room to serve everyone tea.

The visitors had taken their helmets off and left their rifles at the door, under the supervision of two of Osborne's soldiers. They sat cross-legged, as best they could, across from their Afghan hosts. The oldest of the hosts had a thick grey beard and a hawkish face. A pair of very dark eyes.

The first part of the *shura* was between Osborne and the Afghans, with Walid translating. How could the Canadians assist in repairing the damage? What other things did the people of Haji Baba need? The hawk-faced elder spoke thoughtfully, affably. Walls could be rebuilt, bullet holes mended . . . The pump in the town square needed fixing. In fact, Haji Baba needed a new well altogether. And also a school. And perhaps a medical clinic.

Osborne nodded along to the translation, making notes in his field message pad. When the elder had finished his list of requests, Osborne asked him if the people of Haji Baba looked favourably on the Canadians and would help them identify any insurgents in the area. The elder smiled mildly and said something.

"He say, 'Of course,'" said Walid.

Right, thought Ryan, looking at the elder's dark, unreadable eyes. Would *panah* have been offered by this man?

"I guess that's about it," said Osborne. "Tell him we're—"

"Just a sec, Sarge," said Pete. "I wouldn't mind having a few words with him."

Osborne blinked. "Ah, well. Okay, sir. But I don't want to hang around here too much longer, especially with that dog and the reporter and whatnot."

Pete nodded. Then he put his hand over his

heart. He said, "Salaam alaikum." He followed this with a string of Pashto words, slow but fluent, by the sounds of it. Ryan caught Pete's name and his own name among the Pashto. They were being introduced to the elder and the other men.

The elder, meanwhile, nodded. It was plain to see that he was impressed. Sergeant Osborne just stared. None of this—whatever it was—had been in his mind for today's little patrol.

After the introductory remarks, Pete switched to English. Walid translated for him. "It's been my pleasure to meet many elders in my job, but I've never met you, so this is a good day. But I haven't met the other elder from your village."

The elder's face gave nothing away. Still the mild smile. He said something.

"He say, 'There is no other,'" said Walid. "'I am the elder in Haji Baba.'"

"That's strange," said Pete. "Someone told me that there was another important man that lived here, but I forget his name."

Now the elder's brow knitted. Just a little. He spoke a few words, and they had a slightly terse edge to them.

Walid cleared his throat. "He say, 'There is no other.' He say, 'If you want to do business, you do business with me.'"

Sergeant Osborne frowned. "Sir, we gotta keep it cool with—"

"This other elder is hard to miss," said Pete. "His eyes are two different colours."

There was a moment of dead silence—and then, abruptly, there was a loud commotion outside. Ryan straightened up, his hand dropping to the pistol on his hip. There was no gunfire, but there was a fair amount of yelling. The elder and the other Afghan men conferred in low voices with each other. Walid couldn't—or wouldn't—translate what they were saying.

Just then the CIMIC second-in-command stuck his head in the doorway. "Sarge? That fuck—I mean, that, uh, *inexperienced* journalist tried to take a picture of some women or kids or something, and now the locals are losing their minds."

"For Christ's sake," Osborne muttered, getting to his feet. "I'm coming. Hey, Captain? I'll get this sorted out, then we gotta get going. We're overstaying our welcome."

Pete waved vaguely at Osborne.

"Carry on, Sergeant," said Ryan.

Osborne shook his head and walked out of the building.

Pete leaned in toward the elder. "You know who I'm talking about."

The elder shook his head. Said something. Frowning, Walid translated. "He say . . . ah . . . he say, '*Ghost.*'"

"Even ghosts have to live somewhere," said Pete.

Outside, the yelling simmered down. Every instinct Ryan had told him to look outside, just to check on the situation, but he couldn't pull himself away from the surreal exchange that was happening right in front of him.

The elder said something, not much more than a whisper. "'Not here. In the Kandahar City,' he say," said Walid.

Pete sat back, steepling his fingers together. He did not take his eyes away from the elder's.

"Care to share?" said Ryan.

Pete did not reply.

# 4

THE CHILDREN BROUGHT HIM JOY. It had
been a long time since he'd known joy; long enough
that he'd believed his heart had hardened to a rock
inside his chest. But these two girls—with the way
they laughed and clutched each other and boldly
looked at him—made him feel almost like a child
himself. It was silliness, of course, the musings of
an old man who had only a handful of years left.
Not even that long, perhaps.

He was sitting cross-legged in the living room
of his son's house. The windows and doors were
shuttered. He opened his arms and the girls came
to him and he squeezed them to his sides. They
squirmed, laughing, and he laughed with them.
The Quran taught that girl-children could shield a
good parent from hellfire; the old man, holding his
granddaughters to his sides, almost believed it was

true. He didn't know for certain, but he knew he'd had at least six decades on the earth. And many of his years—most of them—were soaked in blood.

A lifetime ago the old man's father and his uncle Abdul, both long dead now, had dealt in carpets in Kandahar City. There was a good big house with an orchard, a shop, and business connections in Pakistan. The old man himself had studied at Kabul University. He'd returned to his father's house in Kandahar in the year 1979 . . .

Two months before the Soviets invaded.

The Soviets had built their puppet state and had ruled with iron fists. Middle-class merchants like the old man's father were labelled *bourgeois*, a word the old man had learned in university. The entire family ended up in a miserable camp outside Quetta, in Pakistan. They'd fled Kandahar with what possessions they could carry with them—little more than the clothes on their back.

From Quetta the old man followed a tide of others like him, furious and displaced, to Peshawar, where he'd thrown in his lot with the Hezb-i Islami Khalis network. Before long he was back in the place of his birth, waging jihad against the Soviet infidels. *And kill them where you find them,* the Quran taught. *And turn them out from whence you have been turned out.*

At that moment the three women of the house came into the living room, bearing trays of rice and lentils and yogurt and strips of goat meat, and, of course, the dented teapot. One of the women chastised the little girls for harassing their grandfather. The girls pulled out of the old man's embrace and went to help lay out the meal—but they both gave him sly smiles when he looked at them.

Abdul entered from outside. He seemed fretful and agitated, a little more so than usual. "Father," he said, "we should speak in the *hujra*."

The old man shook his head. "No, let's speak here. Sit and eat."

In the earliest days of the old man's time as a muj, he'd been fighting in Sangsar in a *tanzim* led by a quietly fervent man named Mohammed Omar. They'd both been severely wounded in one skirmish—shrapnel from an RPG had shredded one of the old man's calf muscles and had taken out one of Mohammed Omar's eyes. It was during his recuperation, back in Quetta, that the old man's father arranged for him to marry a girl from a prominent Hotaki family. She was long dead, just like so many others he'd known, carried off by tuberculosis, but she'd given him his only son . . .

His only son, who was now pacing back and forth.

"Sit," the old man repeated.

Abdul continued pacing for a moment. Then he lowered himself to the floor. He idly finger-brushed the hair of one of his daughters. He said, "Noor says the ISAF soldiers have left. They . . . they asked about you."

The old man nodded. He was not surprised. Since the *panah* he'd offered, he'd expected something like this. In the eighties, the Soviets had been cruel, mindless tyrants. Shortly after they'd finally given up and left, their tails between their legs, they'd been replaced by every self-appointed warlord from Spin Boldak to Bamiyan. Then a few years later came the black-clad students of the one-eyed Mohammed Omar, the old man's own former comrade. Omar's students might have been tolerable if it weren't for their insipid, joyless fanaticism. The old man had had no use for them then—despite his fighting alongside their leader in Sangsar—and he had no use for them now.

These latest foreigners, with their satellites and

aircraft and night vision and computers, had good intentions, the old man supposed. They came with a great deal of money. While much of the money disappeared into the coffers of the new generation of warlords, some of it ended up in the villages where it was needed. But they were foreigners all the same, and they knew nothing of the true nature of Pashtunwali. The old man wouldn't let the foreigners die like dogs in his home, but neither was he interested in interacting with them.

"I don't care about the ISAF soldiers," said the old man. He did not intend to say it sharply but it came out that way. Abdul cast his gaze to the floor. The little girls looked at the old man with wide, startled eyes. He widened his own eyes and wiggled his brows until both girls broke into grins again. In a softer tone, the old man said, "I will leave here at nightfall. Call Ghulam in the city. Tell him to come and get me."

"I thought you would stay till tomorrow," said Abdul.

"Better sooner than later," said the old man. "This business needs to be taken care of." He turned his attention to the girls. "But don't worry, little ones, I'll come back for a visit in a few days. You'll probably both double in size again before I see you."

The girls giggled.

"The highway isn't safe at night," Abdul murmured.

The old man just looked at his son, not saying anything. If the Soviets had never succeeded in killing him—and they had tried and tried—then some local thug trying to dig a bomb into the road was nothing to even think about.

He'd been back here for only a few days, and in truth he wanted to leave already. He loved his son and his granddaughters, he loved the joy they brought to his old, wretched heart, but the province of his birth was too haunted for him to ever feel at peace here again. He had returned to Kandahar to settle one account, and one account only. He even intended to settle it without the shedding of blood, if such was at all possible. Then he would return to Peshawar, where he'd made a home in his autumn years, and live out his final days in peace, God willing.

The old man made a silly face at his granddaughters. He doubted they could shield *him* from hellfire, and he knew he would never see them grow up to become women.

# 5

THE AFGHAN MAN WAS CLEANING the rug with a carpet-beater made out of stiff metal wire. He held the rug in one hand and pounded it mercilessly with the other. The dust exploded from the fibres and hung bright and golden in the late afternoon sunlight. Pete, sitting in a crooked plastic deck chair and smoking a cigarette, watched the cleaner with tired amusement.

Surrounding the men were ugly stacks of scrap metal—mostly the remains of derelict Soviet aircraft, stripped to their frames and thick with rust. A heavy odour of old machine grease and metal hung in the air, cut only by the smell of Pete's cigarette. This semi-secret scrapheap, tucked in behind the KAF airport terminal and enclosed by high walls and chain-link fence, was known as the Boneyard.

The chair Pete was sitting in was in the shade of an abandoned Maersk sea can. Pete had "claimed" the sea can—he'd hung a heavy chain and padlock across the doors and put some busted furniture in the interior—early in his tour, and he came out to it whenever he needed to conduct business. Certain kinds of business, especially in Kandahar, benefited from the privacy of the Boneyard.

Pete watched the cleaner beating the rug for a few more seconds, long enough to finish his cigarette. Then he said, "Haji, what the hell are you doing?"

The cleaner smiled brightly. "The rug is dusty."

The cleaner was a lean man with high cheekbones and a thin black beard. There was an Asiatic slant to his eyes; Pete guessed the cleaner was at least part Hazara. Pete had no idea where the man had learned English, but he spoke it almost perfectly. Hanging from a strap around the man's neck was a plasticized KAF ID card.

"The entire country is dusty," said Pete. "Step into my office. We'll have some tea."

At that moment a couple of A-10s, lifting off from the airstrip nearby, roared past overhead. The A-10s were fairly low, and in their wake a fresh cloud of dust lifted from the ground. The cleaner stood there, still holding the rug, blinking rapidly. His wide grin did not falter.

Pete pitched his cigarette out and stood up from the plastic chair. He opened one of the sea can's doors and led the way inside. The interior walls of the sea can were panelled with dry, splintery plywood. There were a few more plastic chairs and a Coleman lantern. The cleaner brought the rug back in and composed it carefully on the floor. Then he sat down, crossing his legs beneath him.

Pete had come with a small backpack. Out of the backpack he produced a thermos of tea. He filled two paper cups and gave one to the cleaner. Then he set out half a dozen stale Oreo cookies on a paper plate. There was business—the Boneyard kind of business—to conduct, but first there must be hospitality and conversation.

"How is your time, Pete?" said the cleaner. "How is your family?"

"They're good," said Pete. "I talked to my wife a couple days ago. She gets used to not having me around. She put a new sink in the kitchen. Hooked up the pipes and everything. Anyway, how is your family? Will you get up to Kabul soon to see them?"

"Soon, inshallah."

"Inshallah," said Pete.

A few moments of companionable silence passed. They each ate a cookie and sipped their tepid tea. It had been two days since Pete had returned from Sperwan Ghar. He'd had a lot of his normal work to do—the routine slate of daily meetings, one after the other, broken only by the never-ending reports and slideshows to put together on Lieutenant-Colonel Armstrong's behalf—but on the side he'd been making inquiries through his own network.

As if on cue, the cleaner's smile faltered a little and his Hazara eyes narrowed. "Pete, my friend, I thought you were crazy."

"Oh yeah?" said Pete, keeping his tone casual.

"But maybe I was wrong," said the cleaner. "I don't like to be wrong."

"So. I'm not crazy."

"My cousin says he is here," said the cleaner.

"In the city?"

"My cousin thinks so."

Pete leaned back. He could feel his pulse accelerate. His hands had suddenly become moist. He rubbed his fingers together and forced himself to take a slow, steady sip of tea. "Is your cousin sure that it's him?"

"The eyes, my friend," said the cleaner. "My cousin saw the eyes."

Pete forced his way through another sip of tea. He swatted a fly away from the plate of cookies. Keeping his voice steady, he said, "Can you get me to him?"

The cleaner grinned again. "I have already asked. And I believe it is so. The old man has no interest in ISAF, but he will meet as a favour to my uncle. Can you come to the city—not tomorrow, but the day after?"

"Yes I can," said Pete. "But let your cousin and your uncle know I'll have somebody else with me. A friend."

The cleaner nodded. "I will make the phone call. Why do you think he has come back here?"

"I don't know," said Pete. "But I'm aiming to ask him."

"Okay," said the cleaner.

Pete finished the rest of his tea and then dug into his backpack. "I got some stuff for you, by the way. Some more of that shampoo you're all crazy about. And the hand cream."

He handed a couple of plastic containers of Dove men's shampoo and Nivea moisturizer to the cleaner. The cleaner accepted these offerings as if they were bars of gold. The grooming products disappeared into his shalwar kameez. "Thank you, my friend."

"You need anything else, Haji?"

"I am good."

"You always say that."

The cleaner shrugged. "I'm an Afghan."

Both men laughed, but then the cleaner's face became shadowed and contemplative.

"What's wrong?" said Pete.

"I don't know for certain. But there is trouble in the city. Maybe and maybe not relational—"

"Related."

"Yes, related."

"What trouble in the city?" said Pete.

"There is talk. An attack. A big attack. For the Taliban to show how strong they are."

"I've heard some rumours on my side," said Pete. "Do you think it's for real?"

"I do not know," said the cleaner. "If I find out

more, I'll tell you. But, my friend, when you come to the city, take extra care. Okay?"

**- - -**

Kandahar City, thought Ryan. Fuck.

It was true that the provincial countryside held some fascination for him. The hard vegetation, the long vistas, the ancientness of everything. But Kandahar City was much different. It was ugly, filthy, crowded. Half the buildings had been falling down for a long time; the other half, newly built, were falling down in short order. And there were stinking, open-air sewage ditches everywhere. He *hated* the city.

Not surprisingly, being sent to the city had something to do with Pete Mitchell. That patrol to Haji Baba a few days ago had been intriguing, but as far as Ryan could tell, it had come up empty. Since then, the elder with the crazy eyes had become less and less tangible. There were more immediate issues for Ryan to worry about.

He was packed to go, but he hadn't left Sper yet. At present he was in the snipers' weather haven near the company CP. He had some maps laid out on a six-foot table. All four of his sniper detachments were standing around the table. A couple of the boys were drinking coffee or pop; a couple were chewing tobacco and spitting into empty water bottles.

"Okay, guys, listen up," said Ryan. "All four dets are out tonight. Observation posts will all observe and report only. Except for you, Trav. You've got Six-Six, and you'll be back on Hyena where that fucking bend is. So keep your eyes peeled."

Across the table, Travis just nodded. Ryan had privately filled him in on everything already, over breakfast.

"Are we losing you or something, Warrant?" said Tank.

"Yeah," said Ryan. "I'm hitching a ride on a CLP up to KC for a day or two. I've been attached to higher's effects shop."

"What, some hearts and minds bullshit?" said Hickey.

"Something like that," said Ryan.

He'd been advised about the tasking late the night before, at a company orders group in the CP. Jenn had told him, and since it was in front of everybody else, all the platoon commanders and the company sergeant major and the signallers, she'd been brisk and businesslike about it. She'd called him Warrant Murphy. The rest of the orders group was focused on some very bad news—a couple of American guys had gotten captured.

Later, as the group dispersed, Jenn had spoken to him in a relatively quiet corner of the room. *Sorry to drop that on you, Ryan. I just got it from higher. I pushed back, but Lavigne wouldn't bend.*

*Okay*, was all Ryan replied.

Just then, there'd been need in her eyes. Real vulnerability. Maybe learning about the captured Americans had upset her. But before anything could be said, she'd turned around to study something on the battle board. That was that.

Ryan cleared his throat. He found he wanted some of his guys' chewing tobacco. He hadn't dipped in a few years, but sometimes the craving came back hard. He said, "Uh, where's Wilf?"

Corporal Wilf Strauss stepped smartly to the edge of the maps. Wilf was only a few weeks in theatre. He wasn't much older than twenty-one or -two. His sniper qualification was brand new. "Yes, Warrant?"

"You'll be stepping up in my det, bud," said Ryan. "Talk to Trav—to Master Corporal David-son—when we're done here."

"Yes, Warrant," said Wilf.

"For Chrissakes," said Hickey. "Relax a little, will you?"

Ryan straightened up, almost giving in to the urge to ask for some chew. "There's one more thing. I got this last night at orders. A couple of American guys from 10th Mountain got cap-tured."

An uneasy quiet filled the room.

"Say again, Warrant?" Tank said in a lowered voice.

"Yeah," said Ryan. "I don't know the details, but there was an IED attack of some kind, out in Maywand near the Helmand border. Things got confused and the Taliban grabbed two of them."

"Alive?" said Travis.

"Yes."

The funereal quiet endured for a second or two longer, and then Hickey abruptly kicked over one of the chairs. "Fucking savages! Blow me up with an IED, shoot me with an AK, fuck-ing run me over with a LAV—I'm fine with that!

But do not let me be taken alive by those god-damn medievalists."

"What would they do to you?" said Wilf.

"It's unspeakable," said Tank.

"What do you—?"

"Hey, bud," said Travis. "Unspeakable means we don't speak about it."

After the snipers were dismissed, Travis hung around for a few minutes. He didn't say anything, just stood there waiting for Ryan to speak.

"I gotta get going," said Ryan, rolling up a map.

"You all right, Ry?"

"Yeah."

"Any change with Jenn?"

Ryan had told Travis everything. The two of them had been friends for many years. But right now he didn't have the time or the energy to do much more than shake his head.

Travis nodded. "Well, anyway, do you have any idea what this batshit captain is after?"

Ryan started to say something. Then the word *ghost-hunter*, like one of those stupid paranormal reality shows back home, came into his mind. He smiled sourly. "Yes. No. I don't know."

"Well, be safe."

"It's Kandahar City," said Ryan. "Worst thing is if I trip and fall into one of the sewage ditches. *You* be safe out on Hyena tonight, brother."

- - -

A large Kuchi camp was spread across a broad plain on the western outskirts of the city. The camp was packed with tents and people; these nomads were as ragged as the patchwork hovels they lived in. There were camels among them. A mixed herd of goats and sheep. Everywhere, discarded plastic bags swirled and dipped on the breeze. The sun overhead was cruel. The air, this close to the city, was smoggy and thick.

In a gritty vacant lot at the edge of the Kuchi camp, Pete was waiting. He was wearing his helmet and vest, had his pistol and C7, and was sitting in the passenger seat of a beat-up, unmarked Ford Ranger. His friend the cleaner was dozing in the seat behind him. There were two other Rangers in Pete's group, each full of ANA troops. The Rangers had blacked-out windows; at a glance, no locals would be able to tell which of the countless local factions—everything from the ANA to the

Taliban to Bashir Daoud Khan's private militia—these vehicles belonged to. Also, the edge of the Kuchi camp was a good place to park for a little while. The nomads, already outcast from Afghan society, tended to be left alone.

Pete glanced at his watch. 12:35. A little over half an hour until the meeting.

The ANA driver said something. Pete looked up. A hundred metres away, a small convoy of Canadian logistics vehicles, escorted by a pair of bulky RG-31s, was slowing to a halt. The convoy had come from the southwest. Dust swelled and rolled around each of the vehicles' tires. Half a dozen Canadian soldiers dismounted from the vehicles and formed a local cordon. They were separated from the Kuchis by a moderate distance; the Kuchis did nothing but stare impassively from the confines of their rundown camp.

"Better late than never," Pete muttered. He opened the passenger door and stepped down from the Ranger.

One of the Canadians, carrying a daypack and a C8, was emerging from the cordon, coming Pete's way. Pete offered a little wave. Ryan nodded in return.

"Good to see you," said Pete, shaking Ryan's hand. "Any issues coming up from Sper?"

"We were stopped for an hour on Hyena while some engineers cleared an IED out of a culvert," said Ryan.

"You can't be too cautious down that way. Every day we fix Hyena, every night they put bombs into it."

"I'm here now," said Ryan. "Is this our ride?"

"It is," said Pete.

"It's all pretty secret squirrel," said Ryan.

Pete chuckled. "I like keeping a low profile. Ready?"

Ryan nodded. He thumbed the switch on his MBITR. "Eight-One Delta, this is Sunray Six-Six. I'm good here. Thanks for the lift. Out."

The dismounted Canadians in the cordon around the logistics patrol started to collapse back to their vehicles. Pete got back into the Ranger. Ryan clambered into the back seat, setting his daypack down on the floor of the cab.

The cleaner had woken up. He smiled his bright smile, offered Ryan a handshake. "Hello, my friend."

"How's it going," said Ryan, shaking the cleaner's hand. "Hey Pete, you trust these guys?"

Pete tapped the ANA driver and nodded for him to start driving. He said, "Yes I do. I trust them with my life. It's their war a million times more than it's ours."

- - -

The unmarked Rangers moved with the logistics patrol into the heart of the city. The traditional mud-brick compounds gave way to shabby mid-rise edifices of concrete and mirrored glass, everything dun-coloured or soot-stained, connected by tangles of electrical and telephone wires. At street level, shops and storefronts were jammed into every possible opening. Merchants were shilling fruit and produce and cellphones and cheap electronics and engine parts. Vehicles of all descriptions lined the road: garishly decorated jingle-trucks, little Toyota compacts, autorickshaws, motorbikes, and even the odd buckboard wagon being pulled by a donkey. The civilians were mostly men or boys, almost all dressed in shalwar kameez, all stolidly going about their business. Afghan cops were posted on every second or third corner. These local cops looked even motlier than the ANA.

The logistics patrol maintained a steady pace along the main drag. All the locals knew to get out of the way of ISAF vehicles. If a civilian car came too close, the escalation-of-force procedure would start with a warning shot through the engine block—and go up from there, usually in a matter of seconds. The Rangers, taking advantage of the parted traffic, stayed close to the logistic patrol's rear vehicle.

In the middle of the city was a massive asphalt roundabout. It was here that the logistics patrol broke off to the southeast, bound for KAF. The three Rangers curved around the ugly concrete fountain in the centre of the roundabout, negotiating the sudden enclosure of traffic, before following a wide boulevard to the north.

A short distance farther on, the cleaner leaned up and tapped Pete on the shoulder. "It is good here, Pete."

"Okay," said Pete.

He nodded to the ANA driver. The driver slowed the Ranger to a crawl. The sea of pedestrians and motorcycles and auto-rickshaws swelled in on either side. In one fluid motion, the cleaner opened his door and hopped out and closed the door behind him. Almost immediately he vanished into the crowd.

"So who is that guy?" said Ryan.

"He's a cleaner on KAF," said Pete.

"A cleaner on KAF," Ryan echoed.

"He's a good friend of mine, if that makes sense," said Pete. "But we can't really be seen together, if you know what I mean. His family's in Kabul. As far as I know he hasn't seen them or slept in the same bed more than three nights running in over two years."

"Why?" said Ryan.

"Why what?"

"Why do you think your cleaner buddy helps?"

Pete shrugged. "Love of country? I honestly don't know. We pay him but not nearly enough. He's in it for his reasons. You look around, Ryan, every Afghan you see is playing by his own rules. The smartest ones, like my friend, are playing a long game. Understanding that is the foundation of trust with these people, if you ask me. Okay. We're almost there."

The Ranger convoy had turned down a claustrophobically narrow street. It was much quieter here. Shadier. Rubbish blew along the curb. Abruptly each vehicle stopped. Badly tuned brakes squealed. The ANA troops from the other two Rangers piled out onto the cracked and pitted asphalt. The troops took up defensive positions, holding their AKs at the ready. There were far fewer locals here than there had been on the main roads; just a few men who might have been bums or heroin addicts or just civilians squatting birdlike in the shade. These men watched the ANA impassively.

Ryan and Pete got out of their Ranger. They were joined by the interpreter, Walid, who'd been in one of the other trucks. Pete took a small olive-drab backpack out of the passenger side footwell and slung it over one shoulder. Here, the stench of the city air was cut by a more pleasant smell—the aroma of baking bread. Pete pointed to a storefront at the end of the narrow street. There were glass windows with neatly kept frames, all painted pale blue. A prodigious amount of naan was hanging from metal racks behind the windows. A signboard over the door had script in both Pashto and English; the English read, *Mr. Ghulam Kandahari Bakery*.

"Let's go," said Pete.

They walked the short distance to the bakery. Pete led the way through the front door. The interior was dusky and very hot. Woodsmoke and the smell of baking dough hung in the air. The floor was covered with rugs and giant cushions of red velvet. In one corner the rugs surrounded a glowing firepit. A pair of red stage curtains—the same velvet as the cushions—concealed an interior doorway on the far wall. Somewhere a radio was playing Bollywood pop music. The proprietor of the joint was a slender, gap-toothed man, pretty well indistinguishable from every other local. He appeared to be the only person in the joint.

"Salaam alaikum," said Pete, removing his helmet.

"Wa alaikum salaam," the proprietor said, smiling, gesturing for them to sit down.

Pete shrugged off his backpack and set it on one of the cushions. Then he lowered himself to the rugs. He put his helmet on the floor beside him and leaned his C7 up against the wall. Close to hand if needed—but not too close. He made a point of sitting with his back to the front door. He could sense Ryan's hesitation. "It's okay," he said. "We're guests."

Ryan muttered a word of protest but then also sat down and took off his helmet. The sniper sat with his back to the wall and his C8 only inches away. Walid lowered himself to the floor on Ryan's left side.

The proprietor squatted down near the firepit. With a set of steel tongs he removed two naans. He offered one to Pete and one to Ryan. As soon as they'd accepted the bread, the proprietor jumped to his feet and set about pouring tea from an ornate silver pot. Once the tea was poured into a pair of glass mugs, the proprietor slipped through the red curtains and disappeared.

Pete swallowed a mouthful of naan. "That hits the spot. I'd take this over the DFAC any day."

Ryan looked a little doubtful. "What now, Pete?"

"Well, we wait and—"

"Hello, my friend."

The Canadians looked up. The cleaner was coming through the red curtains, grinning his bright grin. He sat down on the rugs. A second later, the curtains parted again. Standing in the opening, the old man regarded them with his very different-coloured eyes.

---

Despite the heat inside the bakery, Ryan was oddly chilled. He kept waiting for the old man to morph into someone else, or else to vanish completely. It was almost as if this were an illusion. A fever dream of some kind. But two seconds passed, then five seconds, and the old man was still there, placidly looking at the Canadians. The bakery still smelled like naan; there was still sweat rolling down Ryan's back. He felt Pete's eyes on him.

"It's him," said Ryan.

Right away, Pete started talking in Pashto. "*Sta-lay-ma-shai. Sang-i-yea. Jor-ya, pack-air-ya, shi-yam. Man-nan-na. Du-sha-coor. Sam nam a Pete-yem. Zma Turfi-mon Walid e zma comrade Ryan-ya.*"

The old man stepped into the room. There was that slight limp in his right leg again. Despite the limp, he lowered himself to the rug. He sat with his legs crossed and his back perfectly straight and his hands loosely clasped together.

Switching to English, Pete said, "This naan is very good. And this is my friend, Ryan. We have known each other and loved each other a long time. Our families know each other. You helped my friend Ryan in the village of Haji Baba."

Walid translated into rapid-fire Pashto. The old man gave nothing away. He did not take his eyes off the soldiers. Ryan felt fresh sweat break out under his combats.

"I would like to repay you for your kindness," said Pete. "I am sure you have something that needs building. A culvert, new rugs for your mosque. I would like to help you with that."

Walid translated. Still nothing from the old man.

Pete leaned over to Ryan. "Pass me my bag, will you?"

Ryan reached into the corner and retrieved Pete's patrol pack and passed it to him. He watched as Pete opened the pack. Ryan's breath caught in his throat. The inside pocket was stuffed with bundles of American hundred-dollar bills. Pete withdrew a couple of the bundles.

"Jesus," said Ryan. "How much is that?"

"I don't have a clue," said Pete. "Welcome to the world of effects."

Pete set the money on one of the velvet cushions. The faintest of smiles touched the sides of the old man's mouth. In slow, halting English he said, "Only a fool accepts gifts without knowing what they are for."

Pete nodded. "Perhaps you can tell me something. I have heard of a legendary warrior, a mujahedeen in the jihad against the Soviets. Among other things, this man was called the Lion of the Desert."

"I have also heard of this name," said the old man.

"The word is he's resurfaced, that he's once again mujahedeen," said Pete. "Do you know these rumours?" The old man did not reply. The faint smile had faded from his lips and his face was once again unreadable. After a moment, Pete said, "May I ask where you are from?"

The old man spoke in Pashto again. Walid translated: "He says his village is called Abdullah Jan."

"Really?" said Pete. "So you're Pakistani."

The elder shrugged and replied. Walid translated: "He says he has been Pakistani for many years, a Muslim for fourteen hundred years, and a Pashtun for five thousand years."

Pete smiled. "I understand." He reached into a

side pocket on his backpack and came up with a small business card. He offered it to the old man. "If you should happen to hear anything about the Lion, we would greatly appreciate it."

The elder accepted the card but did not look at it. He smiled and offered a shallow nod of his head. Then he stood up and disappeared back through the curtained doorway. The bundles of money on the cushion remained untouched.

Pete took the cash and shoved it back into his pack and zipped the pack up. Then he stood. He turned to Ryan. "Let's go."

■ ■ ■

Outside the bakery, the local guys who might have been bums or junkies had disappeared. Maybe the ANA troops had chased them away. As Ryan and Pete and Walid went back across the narrow street toward the Rangers, Ryan said, "So the guy is Pakistani?"

"No," said Pete. "That was kind of a test. Abdullah Jan's just some ruins across the border from Spin Boldak. Nobody's lived there for a couple hundred years, least of all him."

"So he's not just some guy from a village, either."

"No, he's not. He's the Lion of the Desert."

"And he's also your ghost."

"Well, not *my* ghost. The Soviets called him *Mavka*, Ghost, because they couldn't kill him. They shot him four times, blew him up twice. Each time he'd spirit himself over the mountains or across the Registan into a Red Cross tent in Pakistan. They'd stitch him up and he'd be back on the ground, blowing Russian choppers out of the sky."

They came alongside Pete's Ranger. At a nod from Pete, the ANA troops started to fold back in. At that moment, Ryan realized something was bothering him. He couldn't exactly say what it was. It was as if the sounds of the city had been muted somehow. He shook his head. It was just the meeting with the ghost giving him the heebie-jeebies. Nothing more than that. He climbed into the back seat. Walid climbed in beside him.

A second or two later, they were on the move again. Pete's Ranger was at the rear of the little convoy.

"You just met a very big gun, Ryan," said Pete. "Think Patton or Monty or Rommel. The Ghost beat the shit out of the Red Army. And he was a kid when he did it."

They turned out of the narrow side street onto a wide main street. Through the tinted windows, Ryan watched as a handful of city dwellers went about their afternoon business. If he'd been thinking about what he was seeing instead of the meeting, he would have noticed that there weren't enough city dwellers. The crowd here was too thin. The pattern of life was all wrong.

"When the Russians pulled out in '89," said Pete, "the Ghost cut a deal with the same guys who went on to become the Taliban. Mullah Omar and his students. The Ghost says to them, 'I'm going back to my grape fields, I'm not interested in the Deobandi stuff, leave me alone.' And they did, which was weird, because generally the Taliban went after everyone who stood against them. But him, they left alone. He was a legend even to them."

The Ranger convoy turned a corner. An Afghan police station came into view. It was a newer-looking concrete building, likely built with ISAF funds. A red-and-white striped cinderblock wall, topped with razor wire, surrounded the building. The front entrance consisted of a gate-arm and a corrugated metal guard hut, with the police crest painted on the side. A couple of cops milled about the curb in front of the station.

"Now he's back," said Ryan.

"Yeah," said Pete. "He's back, and I gotta figure out why. A guy like that, with his influence? If we can just, you know, get him into the right room at the right time."

Other than those cops, the sidewalk and street in front of the police station were almost totally deserted. An air horn honked. Ryan saw a flat-fronted Nissan fuel truck barrelling toward the station's front gate in the other lane. He blinked, at last noticing everything. He said, "Pete? Listen. I think—"

The fuel truck turned into a red-orange fireball. The world went black.

- - -

The phone was ringing. Nobody was picking it up. No, it wasn't a phone. It was the endless, high-pitched bell from when Pete had gone to public school. End of recess. Back to the classroom. Jesus fucking Christ, what an annoying sound. Pete's neck hurt. His mouth was choked with dust. That was annoying too, but nothing was as bad as the banshee shriek in his ears.

He opened his eyes slowly. He found it fascinating that the Ranger's windshield was intact—until he realized the windshield was gone altogether. Beside Pete, the ANA driver was also just gone. The driver-side door was open, but the man was nowhere to be seen. Out front, a giant cloud of smoke and masonry dust blocked the street. The silhouettes of people wandered slowly, dreamlike, through the haze. Some of the silhouettes were missing arms. One silhouette was carrying the unmistakable shape of a child.

Something was tapping Pete's shoulder. Someone was talking to him, barely audible through the recess bell. Pete blinked. The tapping on his shoulder, that was Ryan, leaning forward from the back seat. Pete gaped at him. Beside Pete, Walid was blinking slowly. Blood was running out of a gash in his forehead.

" . . . said, you okay?" said Ryan.

Pete nodded. "I think so." His voice sounded small and faraway.

"What's our call sign?"

"Golf Niner Whiskey," said Pete.

Pete watched as Ryan thumbed his MBITR and spoke into his headset: "Zero, this is Golf Niner Whiskey. I have contact. Inside Kandahar City"—Ryan glanced at the GPS on his wrist—"grid Quebec Romeo 628 232. Ah, one times vehicle IED. At least one. No Canadian casualties, but likely multiple civilian and ANA and ANP. Over."

Ryan listened to whatever came back from higher. Pete gave his head a shake, trying to clear it. The urgency of the situation was becoming apparent slowly but surely, as if he were remembering something bit by bit. He caught the sound of something new through the ringing in his ears—the dry rattle of gunfire. He couldn't tell how far away it was.

"Zero, Golf Niner Whiskey," said Ryan. "Understood."

"What . . . what's the word?" said Pete.

Ryan leaned forward again. "Multiple reports of vehicle IEDs across the city. Three police stations, one near the hospital, one near the prison—coordinated attack."

"I'd heard about this," Pete muttered. "Heard this was coming."

"Yeah, well, I should've *seen* it. Jesus. Anyway, Zero is advising us to head to Camp Nathan Smith."

"I can't see the other Rangers," said Pete.

"They were on the other side of the fuel truck," said Ryan. "I don't know what the fuck happened to them. Our driver got blown right out of his seat. I think it's just you and me."

Pete gave his head a sharper shake. His neck hurt, the ringing in his ears was almost unbearable, but the fogginess had almost all cleared out of his mind. There was no telling how messed up the situation in the city was and how much danger he and Ryan were really in. Brief, horrid visions of the Taliban capturing them occurred to him. They had to get moving. He reached over and turned the keys in the ignition. Nothing. The engine must have been disabled. "Bad news," he said.

"We're on foot," said Ryan. "Yeah, I figured. That gunfire is still a ways off, but we gotta get moving. Are you good to go?"

Pete nodded. He started to unbuckle his seat belt.

Ryan thumbed his comms and said, "Zero, Golf Niner Whiskey. Be advised our vehicle is a mobility-kill. We are proceeding to CNS on foot. Two Canadian pers—call sign Murphy and call sign Mitchell—and one interpreter, call sign Walid. Let 'em know we're coming. Fifteen mikes, maybe thirty. Out."

Ryan and Walid hopped out of the back seat and came around to the passenger side and helped Pete out. Pete was a little dizzy, but he thought he could move okay. What other choice was there? He pulled his C7 off the seat and cocked it and put it on safe. Then he grabbed his backpack of money and slung it over his shoulders. Ryan, meanwhile, was readying his C8.

Pete took a moment to study their surroundings. They couldn't have driven the Ranger even if the ignition had been working; the vehicle had been blown against the corner of a building and the rear axle was bent well out of alignment. The driver was still nowhere to be seen, and there was no time to waste looking for him. Ahead of them, the street was still choked with smoke. A dull glow of fire showed through the swirling blackness. On the asphalt around them lay bits of blackened metal and concrete, the melted hull of a truck tire, and a man's arm torn off at the shoulder. Someone was screaming in the distance. There was a rising wail of sirens—multiple sirens coming from many directions. Gunfire in bursts. And overtop of it all that incessant ringing.

Ryan clapped Pete's arm. "I don't think we want to take the main routes. We'll take back alleys and side streets. CNS is west of here, right?"

"Yes. Just keep us on a bearing. I'll know the neighbourhood when I see it."

Ryan led the way into an alley that was no more than a metre across. The trash and litter underfoot was ankle deep. There was nobody in sight, not even a stray dog. Ryan took quick, long strides. Walid followed him. Pete came last, already sucking wind, hating every cigarette he'd ever smoked and every workout he'd ever skipped.

They came to a blind corner in the alley. Ryan shouldered his C8 and cleared around the corner. He gestured for Pete and Walid to come forward. Six metres ahead the alley opened up into a small open-air garbage heap, enclosed on all sides by the backs of crooked tenements. The stench of sun-baked offal was incredible.

"We'll move through there," said Ryan. "See the wider alley on the other side? Take a bound. I'm covering."

"Moving," said Pete.

He hastened forward, rifle up, and came to the edge of the garbage heap. The windows in the tenements were all shuttered, and the silence—except, of course, for the recess bell—was surreal. A thick column of black smoke from beyond the rooftops was rising into the clear air.

Ryan skidded in behind Pete. "Okay, let's—shit."

Ryan grabbed Pete and pulled him down to the filthy, stinking hardpan. Walid had already laid himself flat a metre away. On the far side of the garbage heap, no more than thirty metres away, a single file of men were rushing out of the wide alley and into a narrower opening. Staying flat on the ground, Pete glimpsed black turbans, an assortment of vests and packs and satchels, ammo belts glinting in the sun, AKs, and at least two men carrying RPGs. "They're heading for the police station," Pete hissed. "Follow-up attack. Christ, this *is* big."

Ryan whispered into his headset: "Zero, Golf

Niner Whiskey. I have observation on multiple dismounted hostiles moving through the back alleys, ah, sixty metres west of my last position. Looks like a follow-up attack on the ANP. I will try to avoid detection. Will advise."

They waited until it looked as if the last of the insurgents had passed through the enclosure. Ryan popped up and took a long bound, skirting the majority of the garbage, to the wide alley. Pete covered him, and then got to his feet and took his own bound. Walid fell in behind. Pete thought of Rémi Lavigne in the TOC the week before, talking about the third IED attack on a police station that month, and he thought of what the cleaner had said out in the Boneyard: *There is trouble in the city. An attack. A big attack.* All the signs had been there, but he'd sidelined them. This fascination with the reappearance of the Ghost had consumed him. He wondered if that could be explained to his wife when a military notification team showed up at her door to tell her he'd been killed in some shitty back alley.

Pete and Ryan covered each other down the wide alley. It opened on a small, weedy parkette where a rusty swing set and teeter-totter stood deserted. On the far side of the parkette was a side street lined with shops and stalls, all of them shuttered, not a person in sight. A smoky haze hung in the air, along with a strong odour of burning.

"That alley across the street," said Ryan. "Next to that camera shop. Covering."

"Moving," said Pete.

He stepped out into the parkette—and right away saw the three dead Afghan cops, collapsed in the grass, no more than fifteen metres away. Behind the cops was a Toyota pickup truck. A black-turbaned man sat at the wheel. A man with a Russian machine gun almost as big as his own body was standing on the bed of the truck. A third man, armed with a folding-stock AK, was crouched on the ground, rifling through one of the dead cop's pockets.

The gunner on the truck bed and the man on the ground both stared at Pete. Pete stared at them. Then he was diving down, firing a burst from his C7. Dirt and grass kicked up around the insurgents. The gunner on the truck bed steadied his machine gun against his hip—and then one hole appeared in his throat and a second in his forehead and he toppled backwards. His machine gun thundered straight up.

Pete half-turned and saw Ryan moving laterally across the ground behind him, taking quick, aimed, single shots with his C8. *Pop. Pop. Pop.* The man who'd been digging through the cop's pockets was shot three times in the chest. He slumped to the ground. He'd never done more than stare stupidly.

More shots from Ryan. The glass fell out of the truck's passenger-side window. The man behind the wheel stepped on the gas and the truck lurched forward. The dead gunner fell out of the back. The truck sped away, weaving on a flat tire, and disappeared down the side street.

"You good?" said Ryan.

"Yeah," said Pete, scrambling to his feet. "Covering."

"Moving," said Ryan.

The sniper sprinted forward, crossed the empty street, and took up a position at the mouth of one of the alleys. Pete moved next, with Walid hurrying along beside him. The pain in Pete's neck was gone and his body was surging with adrenaline. He felt almost giddy. The colours and smells of the world around him were too real, somehow. Too vivid. A hard crash would come later, he knew. If there was a later.

They covered each other through another labyrinth of deserted alleys, steadily moving west. Gunfire and sirens remained a constant in the distance in every direction. *Trouble in the city*, Pete thought again. They emerged from a tight squeeze between two buildings and found themselves in a feedlot behind a butchery. A wooden door that had once been painted green was recessed into the back of the butchery. Walid tried the doorknob and shook his head. A chicken coop of wire mesh and wood was haphazardly framed against the far wall. A ripe smell of chicken shit hung in the air.

"Covering," said Ryan.

"Moving," said Pete. He rushed forward to the corner of the chicken coop and took a knee. The birds behind the mesh squawked and shook their feathers. Pete peered around the corner of the coop. He saw a wide laneway leading out to a street and a row of low storefronts. A kid of maybe eleven or twelve was standing in the laneway, holding a bloody hatchet. At the kid's feet was a butchered bird. The kid was watching Pete. His face was solemn and unreadable.

Ryan skidded to a halt. He glanced briefly at the kid before crouching down behind a waist-high cinderblock wall. He took a moment to change out the magazine in his C8. Pete did the same with his own weapon. Walid crouched down behind Pete. The bleeding from the cut on the interpreter's forehead had stopped and a mask of dried blood covered his face.

"Zero, this is Golf Niner Whiskey," Ryan sent. "Sitrep. We engaged three hostiles about five minutes ago. At present, I am at grid Quebec Romeo 499 229." He glanced at Pete. "How far from Nathan Smith?"

"Another ten blocks," said Pete. "This is slow going."

Ryan nodded, thumbed his comms. "We're at least another fifteen mikes to CNS, over."

A burst of AK fire cut the air. Half a dozen clods of dirt were ripped up from the ground less than a metre from where Pete was crouched. He felt needle-sharp fragments spray his cheeks. He rolled back behind the coop, then flattened him-self down. The chickens were shrieking. Another burst of fire and part of the coop disintegrated. Blood and feathers flew through the air.

Pete crawled on his elbows to the other side of the coop. There was a tiny gap between the corner of the coop and the back wall of the butchery. Pete peered through it. Far down the laneway he could see the shapes of two or three men on a shop rooftop across the street. In the middle distance was that kid. The kid was hunkered down against the laneway wall. He still had the hatchet in one hand, and in the other something else. It looked like a cellphone.

Pete rolled back behind the coop. "Ryan, you see that kid?"

Ryan snuck a quick glance over the cinderblock wall. "I see him."

"He's got a phone. He's spotting for the guys on the rooftop."

Three more bursts of AK fire came. More of the chicken coop came apart. Pete pressed himself harder against the ground. If one of the guys on the rooftop had an RPG . . .

"What?" said Ryan.

"He's *spotting*," said Pete. "The kid. For the guys on the rooftop. Do you have a clear shot at him?"

Ryan frowned. "Do I—? I don't shoot kids. I don't give a shit what he's doing."

"So what—" said Pete, before a sustained burst of AK fire cut him off. There wasn't much left of the coop now. The chickens were an eviscerated mess. "So we go back the way we came?"

Ryan seemed to consider it for a moment. Then, all at once, he sprang from his position behind the cinderblock wall and crashed in beside Pete. A withering hail of gunfire immediately followed him, splintering up the remnants of the coop, carving the ground apart. Ryan sprang forward again—this time to the butchery's back door. He hit the door with his shoulder. Then he put his boot into it. The door did not budge. Ryan levelled his C8 a few centimetres away from the rusty escutcheon plate and fired half a magazine through the metal. This time when he kicked the door it flew inwards. Ryan immediately disappeared through. Pete and Walid followed.

The inside of the butchery was rank. A single, low-watt light bulb hung overhead, casting a feeble glow. There was a thick buzzing of flies. Skinned and gutted sheep hung from the ceiling. An older kid, maybe eighteen or nineteen, was crouched against the wall, holding up a huge butcher knife. Ryan pointed his carbine at the teenager. Without a word the kid dropped his knife and fled through the back door. The two men weaved around the carcasses, making for the front of the shop. Sunlight came in through dirty windows.

It was a bad situation, and Pete knew it. Going back the way they'd come took them farther away from Camp Nathan Smith—and closer to the coordinated attack they'd fled in the first place. Going down the laneway meant being enfiladed, under direct fire from the men on the rooftop across the street. That kid with the hatchet and the phone, spotter or not, would almost certainly be killed in the crossfire. The interior of the butchery gave them a moment's shelter, but it wouldn't take long for the men on the rooftop to figure out where they'd gone, and it was a good bet the front door was in plain sight of the rooftop. One RPG through the glass would be the end of it. Ryan had to know the risks of the situation as well, but he was doing *something*, pressing them forward. At least there was that.

Gunfire. The windows in the front of the

butchery shattered. That didn't take long, Pete thought bleakly. Ahead of him, Ryan didn't stop moving. Pete realized Ryan meant to sprint right across the street, firing on an upwards angle. Pete considered changing magazines, but what did it matter?

Suddenly a hideously painted jingle truck screamed to a halt in the street outside. Any closer and the truck would have torn off the front of the butchery. It took Pete half a second to recognize the elaborate mountain scene painted on the side of the truck's cab. He'd seen it before. Ryan was pointing his C8, about to fire through the cab. Pete grabbed the barrel and pushed it down.

The passenger door was kicked open from the inside. The cleaner looked at them from the seat above. He laughed crazily. "Found you, Pete!"

Walid went first. Then Pete rushed forward, climbing into the cab. Ryan followed. As Pete started to haul the sniper up, the cleaner hopped back behind the wheel and stepped on the gas. Two bullet holes appeared in the roof of the cab, letting in thin beams of daylight. The bullets punctured the dusty leather bench seat between Pete and Walid. The cleaner laughed again and weaved the truck hard to the left, then the right. Pete pulled Ryan the rest of the way into the cab and reached across him and pulled the passenger-side door closed.

The sounds of gunfire got fainter behind them. The cleaner stopped the weaving but did not let his foot off the accelerator.

"Haji," said Pete. "How in the hell did you find us?"

The cleaner did not reply, but he did lean his head out the driver-side window to holler in Pashto at a motorcycle driver in front of them.

Ryan struggled into a sitting position. He thumbed his comms. "Zero, Golf Niner Whiskey. Be advised, we are now moving east in, ah, in a civilian vehicle. Will confirm arrival Nathan Smith. Out." As soon as he'd let off the PTT switch, he said, "I might just puke right now. I don't know."

"That kid," said Pete. "With the phone. Jesus Christ."

The cleaner just laughed.

- - -

Camp Nathan Smith was in the heart of Kandahar City. At one time it had been a fruit warehouse complex, but it had been retrofitted by the ISAF and surrounded by watchtowers and blast barriers. The Canadian provincial reconstruction team made it their home, as did a small number of Americans and Brits. It was ordinarily a comfortable place: two dining facilities, a gym, even a swimming pool in a small water cistern.

But as that afternoon wore on, Camp Nathan Smith was all business. The attacks across Kandahar City had everybody on high alert, either in the camp CP, on the towers, or ready to deploy with the quick-reaction force. Beyond the walls, columns of smoke stood into the sky from six different places across the cityscape. The sounds of sirens had not stopped.

At sixteen-thirty, Ryan found himself alone in one of the dining facilities. He was in the same combats he'd worn all day. The fabric was filthy and stinking and would probably have to be destroyed. He had his C8 slung over his back. An American Humvee platoon was destined for Sperwan Ghar from Nathan Smith later that evening, to deliver mail and rotate some of their soldiers out; Pete had arranged for Ryan to ride along. He had no desire to spend another minute in Kandahar City.

He poured himself a cup of coffee. Then he wandered out of the dining facility. He found himself beside the camp's little pool. There was nobody else around. A couple of magazines and paperbacks had been left on the poolside loungers.

Ryan sat down on a plastic chair. He was troubled, but more than anything he was exhausted. He'd burned a lot of adrenaline that afternoon; utter exhaustion was the price to pay. It was easy, he supposed, to feel as if he'd been caught up in bigger things. Two encounters with the old man called the Ghost now, both accompanied by close-range shootouts. He believed in his own training and skill set far more than he believed in luck or fate, but it was still hard to shake that sense that events were turning around him. That *he* was the lynchpin at the centre of it all.

He swore and dismissed the idea. He'd just got himself caught up in things well above his pay grade, that was all. He was as replaceable— as ultimately insignificant—as the next guy. He wanted nothing more than to go back to his det, join them on overwatch somewhere, and forget all about the Ghost, Pete, Jenn . . . He even believed forgetting was possible.

"Ryan."

Ryan looked. Pete was striding his way across the cement pool deck. Every time this guy appears, Ryan thought, things get fucked up.

"I was in the CP," said Pete. "What a god-damn mess out there. It was organized to shit. Three truck bombs, four suicide bombers, a dozen RPGs, nineteen insurgents dead, same number of cops dead, and about a hundred people injured, most of them civvies."

There was something pensive in Pete's voice—something encompassing anger and respect alike. Certain people were too smart for their own good; Ryan guessed Pete fit into this category.

"Were they after the ANP HQ?"

Pete nodded. "Yeah, that's what it seems like. They couldn't get near it so they went after some of the sub-stations instead. You and I just got caught in the middle of everything. Kandahar karma, baby, that's what that is." He paused to light a cigarette, and then he laughed dryly. "I'd bet my retirement that Bashir fucking Khan gave his blessing on this."

Ryan took a sip of coffee. "You've got a weird job, you know that?"

Pete looked at him, eyebrows raised. "And you don't?"

"No," said Ryan. "With what I do, everybody knows the rules. You pick up an RPG or an AK, you're going to hear about it. There's no grey area. There's none of this, I don't know, behind the scenes shit. Men in bakeries making phone calls or offering each other cash or talking in circles. There's no hearts and minds for me to worry about."

"Hearts and minds is how we sell this back home," said Pete. "The people around here don't want what we're offering, Justin Bieber and Tom Jefferson and pornography and . . . fucking in-ground swimming pools, like this thing here. These people just want our money and a little stability. There's no winning here, Ryan. There's just an end state, and that's up to the politicians, not us. And when it comes to politics, it's the backroom phone calls that make the difference. It's getting the right men in the right room at the right time. Pulling the trigger—that's just the last resort. No offence."

"None taken," said Ryan.

It occurred to him that they were both talking too quickly, their words jumbling out one after the other. That, too, was part of the come-down after the adrenaline rush. Loosened tongues, frayed nerves. Ryan wouldn't say that he and Pete were friends. He wasn't even sure he liked the man, but they'd both come through the breach that day, together. That bonded them in a strange, indescribable way.

Pete glanced at his watch. "I'm jumping on a Griffon back to KAF in about twenty minutes."

"So what happens next?"

"I honestly don't know," said Pete. "There are some calls I need to make, some friends I'll need to talk to. But if I can use you . . ."

"You know where I'm at, I guess," said Ryan.

Pete blew out a stream of smoke. He offered a handshake. "Take it easy down there on Hyena Road, Warrant."

# 6

THE NIGHT SKY OVER HYENA ROAD was cloudless and profuse with stars. A three-quarter moon cast a silver glow over the asphalt and surrounding scrubland and grape fields. A long distance to the northeast, the lights of Kandahar City combined in a hazy, artificial corona. Events in the city had been wild and violent that day. By contrast, the long and empty stretches of southern Panjwayi seemed peaceful. It was almost believable that the insurgents had left this part of the world alone for one night. Almost.

At a little before twenty-two hundred hours, a small white compact car with flickering headlights came to a stop along Hyena. A short distance from the front of the car was that same big V-shaped notch in the hardtop, still packed with loose gravel and sand.

Three men stepped out of the car. In the moon-light it was impossible to tell the colour of their shalwar kameez; the men were lithe and spectral. Two of them popped the car's hood. One of them tinkered with the engine. The second man held a feeble light—maybe a cellphone—for his mate to see by.

The third man went around to the back of the car. Lifted the trunk lid. Withdrew a shovel and a plastic cooking-oil jug. The jug was bound with what appeared to be duct tape and an ugly snarl of wires. The man, moving like a wraith, carried the jug over to the notch in the road and set it down. Then he put the shovel to the gravel, planting the blade with one rubber-sandalled foot . . .

He never heard the bullet that tore his head off above the jaw. It was almost a full two sec-onds before the sound of the gunshot followed. By then the other two men were already moving. One man was bounding down the road. He was shot mid-stride. He spun halfway around and dropped kicking into the ditch by the side of the road.

The remaining man, preserving some frag-mentary sense of self-preservation, had dropped into a prone position. He crawled on his belly and elbows back towards the car. The third bullet took him just above the knee, almost severing his leg altogether. He stopped moving. The blood pooled around him, as black as oil.

- - -

"Three Niner Alpha, this is Six-Six Delta," said Travis. "Three times enemy engaged. I assess all three are KIA. We're exfilling now, over."

Captain Bowman's voice came back: "Six-Six Delta, acknowledged. See you soon. Out."

The snipers' hide, this time, was in the shadow of an abandoned, roofless building seven hundred metres south of the road. Travis, Tank, and the new guy, Wilf, were already packing up their gear and weapons. Hickey was off to one side, pulling something out of his ruck.

"Hickey," Tank whispered. "We're outta here, man. What the fuck are you doing?"

"I've got to shit first," said Hickey.

"Shit?" asked Wilf. "How come?" The new guy's voice was edgy and agitated. His very first night out with the det, they'd had an engagement.

Now that the position was compromised, the kid was no doubt eager to get the hell out of there.

"Why do I have to shit?" said Hickey. "Maybe because my lower intestine is full of IMP."

"Make it quick," said Travis.

Hickey finished pulling a shit bag from his ruck. He scooted off a few paces and dropped his pants and got to work. Wilf knelt down nearby, keeping watch through the sight on his C8. Travis and Tank settled down against the wall of the abandoned building.

"Beauty of a night," Travis said in a low, thoughtful tone. "If they ever get it sorted out, I'd come back."

"You'd come back here?" said Tank.

"Yeah, I'd take my boy camping. You know, back in the day, the sixties, this was *the* place for all the hippies trying to hitchhike from Europe to India. The local women back then didn't have to cover up or anything."

"You ask me," said Tank, "we should just make this whole place a parking lot."

"Number two is fully off-loaded," said Hickey, hauling his pants back up.

Travis started to stand up. "Okay, let's—"

"Master Corporal," said Wilf, his voice almost shaking. "Our contact's still active."

The snipers all sank to the ground. Tank popped out the bipod on the Tac-50 and Travis brought up the spotter's scope. The gear was all fitted with night-vision adapters; through the strange green-black haze, they could see that the remaining man had not only climbed back into the car, but he'd got it moving again—all with one leg almost severed. The hood and the trunk and the three doors were still open. The man might have made it had he not stalled the vehicle as he was trying to shift to a higher gear. In the few seconds he was halted—no doubt desperately trying to work the clutch and the ignition and the gearshift and the gas—Travis called the gusts and deflection. Tank sighted, readied, stood by.

"Send it," said Travis.

Tank fired. After a split-second's travel time, the bullet smashed through the insurgent's shoulder and chest cavity and exited through his other arm. He died with his forehead pressing the horn. The breeze, although faint, was at just the right angle to carry the sustained car horn to the snipers. The sound was at once mournful and funny.

"Three Niner Alpha," sent Travis. "This is Six-Six Delta. Slight delay. Exfilling *now*."

---

After Six-Six's engagement was complete, Jenn stepped out of the company CP for a breath of the night air. She was exhausted. The attacks in Kandahar City—even though it was forty kilometres away and outside of Charlie Company's area of responsibility—had had everyone on edge since noon. Insurgents either entering or extracting from the city could easily be moving through Panjwayi, quite close to Sper. If that happened, it would become Charlie Company's problem fast. So far the only contact that night had been Six-Six's would-be bombers on Hyena, but as she well knew, nothing in this country could be taken for granted.

There'd also been Ryan to worry about, of course, no matter how much professional distance she'd tried to keep. At fifteen hundred, when word had come from battle group that Ryan had safely made it to Camp Nathan Smith, Jenn had staggered.

Outside the CP, the air wasn't exactly cool, but neither did it carry the stifling heat of the day. She breathed deeply and closed her eyes. It occurred to her that the CP crew—from the signallers to the operations NCO—were all probably taking deep breaths of their own, relieved at her momentary absence. She'd been tough on them all afternoon. Working the CP crew hard was in itself okay, but she'd been *irritable* with them. Her head and stomach had ached, and she'd had two spells of dizziness. She wanted to think the irritability and the aches and the dizziness were nothing more than stress, battle fatigue . . . But now in the quiet of the night she had a sinking suspicion there was something else at work.

"No way," she said aloud.

She turned around. She was about to step back into the CP, but she paused instead. She knew he was there. He was back. She glanced at him. He was just a silhouette.

"Don't say anything," he said. "Just listen to me. I know our situation, I know it makes no sense. But know this from me. I love you. I love you right down to the bone, right down to the god-damned marrow. If I ever doubted that myself—

and I didn't—that clusterfuck in KC today drove it home pretty hard. You need to know it too."

"I do," said Jenn. As she spoke, she felt short of breath. "I do know it."

"I'll keep my distance. I'll keep everything professional from now until whenever we go home. But I had to tell you."

She licked her lips. Her mouth had gone dry. She watched his silhouette walk away. She wanted to call out his name. She wanted to run to him. Instead she tucked it away inside herself, moved back into the CP, and went back to work.

# 7

FOR THREE DAYS, PETE WANDERED KAF in a haze. He went from the battle group TOC to the task force headquarters to the dining facility to the gym to the boardwalk. At night, in his bunk in the modular housing units, he tossed and turned. Some of it was certainly the after-effects of the fight in Kandahar City. He kept reliving the moment the fuel truck exploded, the shapes of mangled bodies through the smoke. The ringing in his ears hadn't gone away, either; it was much fainter, close to inaudible, but it was still there. The damage was probably permanent.

Lieutenant-Colonel Armstrong had offered to give him a couple of days off—to unwind, to see the chaplain or the doctor if necessary—but Pete had declined. He wanted to work. Without work, KAF was as crushingly boring as a penitentiary.

The boredom was sure to make him lose his mind. Besides, thanks to the attacks in the city, there was lots of work *to* do. Analysis after analysis, report after report, PowerPoint slide after Power-Point slide. It seemed that everyone from General Rilmen all the way back to Ottawa needed—*right now*—to know *how* the attack had happened, how ISAF and the ANA and the Afghan cops had been caught off-guard. Wasn't Kandahar City supposed to be safe, relatively speaking, these days? For the time being at least, Rilmen's relentless attention had been pulled away from Hyena Road.

On the third day following the attacks, Pete sat in as a backbencher at a meeting in the task force headquarters. Who else was there, among all the ISAF brass, but Bashir Daoud Khan himself, along with his insipid, gold-toothed son. Khan, receiving a briefing on the civilian death toll from the attacks, clenched his fists and hung his head and vowed eternal revenge on the Taliban. It was theatrical bullshit, of course. Khan had to have known about the attacks well before they started. Pete was certain of that, as were Armstrong and Chewey and everyone else with half a clue. Khan was one of the most powerful "friendly" power brokers in the province; nothing happened without his awareness, if not his direct say-so. The question was what he stood to gain, how the instability and turbulence in Kandahar City lined his pockets.

At the end of the briefing, Khan and his son stood up and began their routine of shaking hands with everyone in the room. "We are your partners in peace," Khan kept saying. Right, thought Pete. Something Chewey had said at the previous meeting occurred to him: *It'd be a fuck of a lot easier to do what we came here to do if Khan stopped breathing for some reason.* If only. But that was impossible, as Pete knew. The house of cards built around him was just too big.

After that briefing, Pete got to work on yet another PowerPoint presentation. This presentation was rich with graphs and tables and different colours. It was bound for Ottawa and was supposed to show how favourable Kandahar City residents felt towards ISAF before and after the attacks. Pete hated making these kinds of presentations at the best of times; right now he could barely force himself through the motions. His thoughts were almost wholly occupied. Not by the attacks and his own part in the fight, however, and not even by Khan.

What Pete Mitchell could not shake was the return of the Ghost.

- - -

A sandstorm was gathering. It hung in the sky to the south, a huge reef of red clouds over the Registan Desert. It looked like some kind of holy wrath from the Old Testament—quite fitting for this ancient country. The sandstorm hadn't hit KAF yet, but most flights had already been grounded in preparation. The air over the base was unnaturally quiet.

Pete stood watching, smoking a cigarette, as the cleaner hosed down the plastic deck chairs outside the Maersk sea can. The hose snaked off somewhere—Pete had no idea where—between the tilting stacks of the Boneyard.

"Haji!" Pete called.

The cleaner pressed his thumb over the hose's nozzle and peered at Pete, smiling. Always smiling.

"What in the hell are you doing?" said Pete.

The cleaner put on an expression of surprise, as if Pete had grown two heads. "Cleaning the chairs, my friend."

"It's not your job. It's nobody's job."

"And that's why you have dirty chairs."

"Right," said Pete. He eyed the south, the gathering sandstorm. Then he turned back to the cleaner. "How about some tea, Haji?"

- - -

They sat inside the sea can, as they had many times before, drinking tea from Pete's thermos and eating Oreos.

"How do you like my hair, Pete?" said the cleaner. "I use the shampoo."

"Your hair is silky and smooth," said Pete around a mouthful of stale cookie. "Very manageable."

The cleaner beamed and ran a hand through the thick coif on his head.

Their lighthearted exchange felt good, but at the same time Pete found it hollow. Insufficient. He simply couldn't find the right words to thank the Afghan for getting him and Ryan out of the butcher shop. He wondered if maybe his gratitude was better left unsaid. Demonstrated, perhaps, if the opportunity ever presented itself.

In the meantime, there were other things to talk about.

"I don't understand why he agreed to see us," Pete said. "He didn't have anything to say, and he didn't accept any money."

It wasn't necessary to be specific; they both knew who Pete meant. The cleaner shrugged. "Maybe he just wants ISAF to know he's back."

"But for what?"

The cleaner shrugged again, but this time offered no reply.

Pete rocked back, leaned against the plywood wall behind him. He didn't know how the Afghans could sit cross-legged or squat on their haunches for hours on end. Thirty minutes cross-legged was enough to give him muscle cramps. "What does he have in the city?" said Pete.

"He has friends," said the cleaner. "Many friends. In the old days, in the war with the Russians, he would sometimes come to the city when he needed a short rest. Safety. But outside the city, that was where he made jihad. In Arghandab, in Maywand, in Panjwayi."

Pete stood up, carrying his mug of tea. He walked to the end of the sea can and leaned against one of the open metal doors to stretch his legs. The air outside had gained a gritty edge. He looked to the south. The sandstorm was closer now. It had consumed the Registan and looked to be halfway across Panjwayi. All those little villages south of Hyena Road would be suffering the storm's wrath at that very moment. Including Haji Baba.

"Why did he first show up down there?" said Pete. "In Haji Baba?"

"I do not know."

"He was in a house . . . It's one thing to have friends in Kandahar City. There are a million places to lie low. But Haji Baba, that's just a wide spot in the road. There's something or somebody there. Who?"

"I do not know, my friend."

Pete gave his head a quick shake and smiled. "I know you don't. Listen. I've asked way too much of you already, but here's one more thing. Do you think you can get into the Tazkera Registry, find out who lives in Haji Baba that might be . . . I don't know . . . special?"

It would have been entirely reasonable for the cleaner to tell Pete he couldn't do it, that he'd done enough for ISAF—for Pete—already. But instead the man was smiling, yet again. Pete couldn't help but wonder what the cleaner's long game was. He doubted he'd ever really know. The cleaner said, "I have an uncle who works in the governor's palace."

"Christ, how many uncles do you have?"

The cleaner made an expansive gesture. "Many uncles."

A tumbleweed cartwheeled past the sea can. "Storm's coming," said Pete. "I guess we better get out of the Boneyard."

A minute later, Pete had the sea can doors closed. He brought the ends of the chain together and secured them with the padlock. The storm was visibly closer now, and coming in fast.

"I will call you," said the cleaner.

"Okay," said Pete.

The two men embraced. When they stood apart, the cleaner offered Pete a handshake. "I use the hand cream too," he said. "What do you think?"

"Very soft," said Pete. "Just like a baby's bum."

The two men shared a laugh before they each hurried off ahead of the storm.

— — —

The dedication ceremony for Hyena Road had been given a name: Operation Open Highway. It had been set for June 20th, less than a week away. General Rilmen had gotten over the attacks in Kandahar City and was refocusing on his central project.

Pete found out about Open Highway when he returned to the intelligence office in the battle group TOC. Staff officers and NCOs at all levels were already busy doing the threat assessments and the planning estimates. Outside, the sandstorm raged. He'd almost made it back from the Boneyard before the storm hit KAF, but he wasn't quick enough. For ten minutes he'd had to jog, head down, while tiny particulates came at him from all sides. Now, sitting in the office, he could feel the grit in his hair and ears and nostrils. He could feel it down his underwear. ISAF urban legend held that a large percentage of the dust during a sandstorm was human fecal matter, given the sheer number of open sewers across the province and all. Pete considered this as he prodded the grit on his teeth with his tongue.

He picked up the desk phone at his work station and dialled the task force intelligence cell.

"ASIC," said Chewey. "Lieutenant Jeffries speaking."

"Chewey, it's Pete. I need a favour."

He heard her laugh. When she replied, her voice was lowered: "Sure you do. When don't you?"

"Yeah yeah, I know. Anyway, I'm looking at a village. Haji Baba, grid Quebec Quebec 413 892. I'm trying to get data on any events in the last, I don't know, say the last six months."

"Is this for Op Open Highway?"

"Sure," said Pete. "Let's say it is."

"Come on, man."

"Look. I know I should go through my boss and yours, but I don't even know what I'm looking for. I don't want to do a full work-up on a hunch."

"You'll want visual, I assume."

"Any eyes you can pull up, yeah."

"I'll let you know," said Chewey. "You might even have to come and visit me."

Just then the office door opened and Lieutenant-Colonel Armstrong came in. Hiding his annoyance at being interrupted, Pete put the phone back down. "Sir," he said.

"You've been hard to find," said Armstrong.

"Running around," said Pete. "You know how it is."

"Open Highway is a go."

"So I hear," said Pete. "It's still pretty hairy down there, sir. Hyena gets IED'd almost daily."

"That's not going to stop General Rilmen. The dedication ceremony is a big deal to him. He wants it front and centre in the public eye. He intends for Bashir Khan to cut the ribbon with him."

"Khan's a goddamn gangster," said Pete. "The Taliban, at least they have their own code, as messed up as it is—but Khan's a vulture."

Armstrong's lips got thin. The man was only a year or two older than Pete, but lately he looked ancient and worn out. Pete guessed Armstrong's mind was focusing more on his upcoming vacation than anything else, but that didn't mean Pete should push him too far. "Khan doesn't matter," said Armstrong. "Anyway, you're talking as if this negates what General Rilmen is planning to do with the dedication ceremony. Which it doesn't. So get on with it, okay?"

"Yes sir," said Pete.

"We'll need up-to-date atmospherics on Hyena, on Panjwayi in general."

"I might need to take the odd reconnaissance down that way," said Pete. What he didn't say was that he might take the odd reconnaissance to Haji Baba as well, if the opportunity presented itself.

Armstrong's eyebrows drooped. His eyes glazed over; he was definitely in a pre-vacation slump. "If you must. Just don't get yourself in another gunfight like you did in KC, please and thanks. Pointy-end gunfighting is not your job."

"I'll do my best," said Pete.

Armstrong nodded and started to leave the office. He paused briefly in the doorway, said, "You're the effects point man on Open Highway, Pete. That means you'll be dealing with General Rilmen directly. He's already got enough on his plate—don't harass him about Mr. Khan. Khan's a gangster, no argument there, but he's ISAF's gangster. Understood?"

"Yes, sir. Loud and clear."

The office door closed behind Armstrong. Pete closed his eyes and ran his hands through his hair and felt sand. Hyena Road, Operation Open Highway, and Bashir Daoud Khan had already all slipped to the back of his mind. Everything seemed eclipsed by the Ghost.

- - -

The various video feeds on Chewey's computer screen showed Haji Baba from far above. Tens of thousands of feet, in most cases. From that height the village looked primeval and oddly delicate. The fields around it seemed to stretch on forever. Some of the imagery came from drones and balloons, some from fast air and satellite. Some imagery was in colour and some in grainy black-and-white. Any people in the frame were nothing more than tiny, antlike blobs.

Chewey had been showing the imagery to Pete for the best part of an hour. It was early morning, and most of the staff of the task force intelligence cell were at breakfast. Just as well that there were fewer people around; Pete and Chewey weren't doing anything *wrong* exactly, but they weren't assisting the planning process for Operation Open Highway, either. Chewey had a tiny, plywood-partitioned workspace. It didn't give her a lot of privacy, but Pete was grateful for what little it did.

The intelligence cell was a kind of inner sanctum inside the task force HQ building. You had to have the requisite security level to enter the cell in the first place—which Pete had—and then you had to leave your cellphone and any other electronic device on a shelf outside the combination-locked door. Inside the cell was a shady, winding warren of computer terminals and servers and telephones. Every square inch of wall throughout was covered in maps and charts and printed-off images of high-value bad guys. There were no windows.

Pete had come with coffee for himself and Chewey both, but otherwise he hadn't eaten yet. His stomach rumbled. He ignored it. "Is this all you got on the village?"

"Almost," said Chewey. "Just a little more. A bit of Predator-porn, actually. You remember Operation Jackal, back in the fall?"

"I do," said Pete.

"Well, here you go," said Chewey.

She clicked her mouse. On her computer screen, video started to stream. It was in colour, but there was no audio. The video showed daytime—morning—by the pale look of the sunlight.

It was not Haji Baba itself but a broad field half a kilometre to the northwest of the village. The field wasn't growing grapes.

"Poppies," said Pete.

"Yep."

The field was not big, no more than a few acres, but the poppies carpeted it densely. As the video progressed, eight men appeared, walking in single file amid the poppies. Whoever had been controlling the drone had decided to zoom in at that point: suddenly the men appeared in a tele-photo close-up. At that level of zoom, it was too blurry to make out their faces, but it was plain to see that each man was carrying a weapon. Pete counted six AKs and two RPGs.

"Up to no good," said Pete.

"Wait for it," said Chewey.

The video zoomed back out to wide-angle. A few more seconds elapsed . . . and then a soundless barrage of artillery turned the poppy field into a gigantic, grey-brown cloud of dirt and smoke that filled the entire frame.

Pete whistled. The video went on for a little while longer, long enough for the smoke to clear. The poppies, for the most part, had been replaced by smoking craters. The insurgents who'd been crossing the field appeared to have been annihilated.

"I'd call that a two-for-one special," said Pete. "The heroin and the bad guys both."

Chewey nodded. "Yep. The BDA was later confirmed by an ANA foot patrol. All eight Taliban KIA." She paused it there. "I don't have much else, but did you get anything useful out of that?"

"I don't know yet. What do I owe you?"

"I'll take your beer allotment at the end of the month."

"Hey, I only get two, same as you."

Chewey smiled sweetly. "And I'll take them both."

At that moment the cell door opened and a couple of officers and senior NCOs came in from breakfast, talking and laughing quietly, carrying coffees. They only glanced at Pete and Chewey as they got to their workstations.

"The beer is yours," Pete said in a low voice. "Thanks, Chewey." He started to go, but then he paused. "Hey, who called in the strike on that field? Was it one of ours?"

Chewey clicked something with her mouse

and squinted at a box of text on her monitor. "Yeah," she said. "Some snipers out of Sperwan Ghar, by the looks of it. Charlie Company guys. Hey—you just got a funny look on your face."

"Did I?" said Pete. "Probably just a twitch. Maybe I took some shrapnel in the head the other day and didn't realize it. Anyway, thanks again. I'll see you."

Pete walked past the other workstations, hands in his pockets. Some snipers out of Sperwan Ghar. It was almost funny. He thought a trip down to Sper might be in order, even if he wasn't sure Ryan would be happy to see him.

As he walked through the intelligence cell door, his stomach rumbled again. He glanced at his watch. He had just enough time, if he hustled, to make it to the nearest DFAC for a lousy but hot breakfast before they closed up to start preparing for lunch. After breakfast he had a shitload of work to do—PowerPoint presentations, what else?—for Op Open Highway. Realistically, he figured, Sper would probably have to wait. Realistically, he would have to put this stuff out of his mind, at least until the stupid goddamn dedication ceremony was finished.

He retrieved his cellphone from the shelf. As he stepped outside the HQ building, he flipped the phone open. Three missed calls, all in the space of twenty minutes. Each call had come from the cleaner. Pete turned in the direction of the DFAC and hit the redial button and put the phone to his ear.

The cleaner answered on the second ring.

"Haji," said Pete. "What do you got?"

Pete, listening to what the cleaner had to say, stopped dead in his tracks. Despite the heat of the morning, he felt cold all over. As of that moment it wasn't a case of maybe going to Sperwan Ghar— it was a case of *needing* to get down there.

# 8

By June 15, the warning orders for Operation Open Highway had made it from task force to battle group and down to Charlie Company. Despite the high profile of the dedication ceremony and the fact that General Rilmen and a bunch of important locals would be attending, Open Highway didn't really change much for Charlie Company; the company's all-encompassing task would simply be to keep the insurgents away from Hyena Road. Situation normal.

Early in the morning, before the day's heat hit hard, Ryan got in a workout at the Sperwan Ghar gym. A lot of soldiers pumped iron, treating their deployments almost like prison sentences, coming home with twenty or thirty extra pounds of solid muscle. It wasn't too hard to get steroids, either, if you knew who to ask. But Ryan didn't have much use for weightlifting or bodybuilding; he stuck pretty religiously to aerobics and long hard runs on the treadmill. Anything to keep his heart and lungs at top capacity. If the hard exfiltration to Haji Baba ten days ago hadn't already proved the value of cardiovascular fitness, the shootout in Kandahar City certainly had.

When he'd finished his workout, he showered. Then he met up with Tank and Travis and Hickey for breakfast in the mess tent. No sooner had he sat down than he saw Jenn in the mess as well, sitting by herself at a table on the far side, eating a bowl of sliced peaches. She met his eye briefly, gave him a quick, reserved smile. Ryan felt his stomach drop. Once seated, he angled himself so that he didn't have to look directly at her.

The only person Ryan confided in was Travis, and Travis was a vault. All the same, people knew about him and Jenn. Of that Ryan was sure. Gossip was like a virus around here. It meant they had been sloppy. Not sloppy enough to get hauled before the chain of command, but who knew how close it had come? The relationship was the only thing Ryan had ever been sloppy about; he'd always prided himself on discretion, orderliness, and having his personal shit wired tight—all vital components of a sniper's mindset—but when it came to her he'd nearly let everything go. It had taken, it continued to take, every ounce of will-power he had to maintain his promise and be nothing but professional.

At least they hadn't had that many interactions. Sperwan Ghar wasn't a big place, but you could disappear into your own corner of it and almost never emerge. Jenn's corner was the company CP; she scarcely ever seemed to come outside it these days. Open Highway, even if it was little more than business as usual for Charlie Company, must be consuming her, Ryan thought.

He tried to lose himself in the typical banter between Tank and Hickey. Beside them, Travis was as quiet and introspective as he always was. Four tables down, some soldiers were singing "Happy Birthday" to one of their mates. The mess's two big-screen TVs were showing baseball highlights from the States. Everything was business as usual. As he scraped up his last morsel of scrambled eggs, Ryan glanced casually in Jenn's direction, but she'd already gone.

---

After breakfast the snipers went over to their weather haven. Nobody was slated to go out until that evening, so Ryan had designated the day for weapon cleaning and other kit maintenance. The interior of the weather haven already had a sharp smell of gun oil. One of the guys had a pirated movie playing on his laptop; four of the snipers, each of them wiping down a bolt or a trigger assembly, were clustered around the laptop, staring like children. There was no limit to the number of movies soldiers on deployment could watch for hours on end. And the movies could be anything—a blockbuster action flick or a cartoon musical, or anything in between. Anything to take you away from the disordered and dangerous reality around you.

Ryan and Travis sat down at the planning table at the far end of the weather haven, with maps spread out before them. The maps were clustered with red marks where they'd had engagements. Most of the red marks, naturally, were along Hyena Road.

"That's where we had the three in the car," said

Travis, pointing with his pen. "The night you got back from KC. Same place where we tagged that guy ten days ago. The Taliban love that spot, but they'll figure out what we're doing, if they haven't already, and start hitting somewhere new."

Ryan nodded. He pointed to a sharp bend in the road. "Maybe here."

"Yeah," said Trav. He tapped his pen against a part of the road that went beneath a steep hill. "Or here."

"Gonna be almost all overwatch jobs for this Open Highway thing," said Ryan. "But we'll have lots of assets, I'm guessing, lots of—"

"Warrant Murphy?"

Ryan looked up from the table.

Wilf Strauss was calling to him from the other end of the weather haven.

"What is it, bud?" said Ryan.

"I just came from the CP. There's some captain looking for you."

"You mean Captain Bowman?"

Wilf shrugged. Ryan sighed. He glanced at Trav, who was thinly concealing a laugh. Ryan got up from the planning table, exited the weather haven, and made his way over to the CP. He went inside. His thoughts were confused. He looked around but Jenn was nowhere to be seen. The CP duty NCO was looking at him, though.

"Where's Captain Bowman?" said Ryan.

"She's over at the medical station," said the NCO.

Ryan blinked. "The medical station . . . ?" He was about to ask why, but he caught himself. It wasn't likely the duty NCO had any idea why Jenn was over at the medical station, and even if he did, he wasn't likely to say what it was. Ryan cleared his throat. "So Captain Bowman wasn't looking for me?"

"Not that I know of," said the duty NCO. "But *he's* been looking for you."

The NCO nodded to someone behind Ryan. Ryan turned around. With a feeling of resignation more than surprise, he saw Pete Mitchell offering him a handshake.

"Warrant Murphy," said Pete. "Good to see you again. I think there's something you can help me with."

---

Ryan had no idea how Pete had gotten out to Sper that morning. It was still fairly early, no later than nine, and he hadn't heard any choppers coming in. That left the road—Hyena Road, as lousy with IEDs as ever.

Pete had his local buddy with him, the cleaner, who had a plastic ISAF tag around his neck, which was undoubtedly how he'd been able to get into Sper. Maybe the two of them had come bouncing down Hyena in the cleaner's hideously painted jingle truck, staying clear of bombers by hiding in plain sight. Ryan couldn't decide whether Pete was brave or completely insane. The latter seemed probable. With all the Pashto Pete spoke and his understanding of Pashtunwali and his local contacts and everything else, Ryan wondered if Pete had—what was the term?—gone native.

Ryan had gone with the two visitors over to the common area. They sat down at one of the crooked picnic tables, in a small patch of shade next to a Hesco wall. It was too hot for coffee or tea, so they each drank from water bottles.

"So what exactly is this help you're after?" said Ryan.

Lighting a cigarette, Pete said, "I'll get to that,

but first I want you to tell me about Op Jackal."

"Don't you already know about it?" said Ryan.

"I want to hear your version. I want to hear what Six-Six did during the op."

Ryan wondered if he was just enabling Pete's insanity. He sipped some water. "Okay, well, this wasn't during fighting season, but the Taliban had all the freedom they wanted to move around down there. Zalukan, Mushan, Haji Baba, everything south of here as far as the Reg. They'd move up from the south and come and go as they liked. They were burying weapons caches and IEDs and shit like that, getting ready for summer. Anyways, we got the orders to clear and hold a—what was the word for it, *corridor*—a corridor twenty klicks long, along the dirt road that was already there. The task force was going to build a fucking highway. But you *do* already know all this, right?"

"I do," said Pete. "But please, indulge me."

Ryan shrugged. "Okay, well, me and all my dets got sent out forty-eight hours ahead of Charlie Company. Mainly we were on recce and confirming civilian pattern of life. My guys put in an OP outside of Haji Baba. We were watching a poppy field. We reported the poppies, but higher wasn't really interested. This wasn't a DEA job or anything like that. Anyways, for twelve hours we kept watch on this poppy field. Saw a farmer come out once or twice and inspect the crops. Then on the morning before the company clearance task was about to start, we spotted a line of insurgents heading north through the field. Half a dozen of them? Ten? I can't remember. Section-sized, at any rate. They were bundled up—it was still pretty cold in the mornings around that time—but they were all packing. A couple had RPGs.

"So we called it in but said there were too many for us to engage directly. Higher came back and told us to keep eyes-on and to put together a fire mission. It was easy; we'd been lazing these guys already and had them down to the ten-figure grid. I sent the fire mission back up, and two minutes later the triple-sevens here in Sper opened up. We didn't do the BDA ourselves, but we didn't need to. There wasn't *anything* moving in that field after the artillery came down on them. There wasn't much of an opium crop left, either."

"That's all?" said Pete.

"More or less," said Ryan. "Since we hadn't put any direct fire down, we hadn't compromised our position. We stayed in place until the end of the clearance task. But it was pretty quiet anyways. We had one of the only engagements of the whole thing. A week or two later they started building Hyena. Then the trouble started."

Pete nodded, looking off in the distance. He stubbed his cigarette out on the top of the picnic table and took a drink of water. The cleaner hadn't said anything at all.

A few quiet moments passed. Ryan finally interrupted it. "So why the hell is this important now?"

"I'm working on that," said Pete.

"Okay, do you want to fill me in? Now?" said Ryan.

Pete didn't reply. Instead he frowned, waving at a fly in front of his face. Ryan glanced around to make sure there was nobody in earshot.

"Look, Pete, every time I see you, there's some kind of massive clusterfuck at work. Seems like we're fighting two different wars. I don't pretend to understand what you do. But now you come all the way out here telling me you want my help. You need to start coming clean."

Pete hopped off the bench. He paced back

and forth on the gravel nearby. "That's fair. Okay. I'll tell you what I know, but it's got to stay quiet for the time being. It doesn't necessarily fit with the overall agenda right now—even if I think it *should*. Does that make sense?"

"Not at all."

Pete waved a hand. "Again, fair. Haji here and I have been doing some digging over the past couple days. Him on his end, me on mine. Here's what we've turned up. Think of that poppy field outside of Haji Baba. You said you observed the farmer, right?"

"Yeah," said Ryan. "Came out once or twice."

"Well, the way it works is, that farmer doesn't own the field. He works it, brings in the harvest, turns the product over to some traffickers, collects the money. At the end of the season he's got to fork over five thousand dollars U.S. to the actual landowner. You know what an indentured labourer is?"

"A slave."

"Pretty much," said Pete. "And that's pretty much exactly what your farmer was. He'd do all the work, and whatever he could make on top of the five grand he was allowed to keep, which was probably like eight hundred bucks, somewhere around the national average. Call it an incentive, a bonus, beyond the usual extortions and threat of violence. Ha ha. Anyhow, in this case, the Taliban go running around in the field, you and your guys call in the fire mission, ISAF blows the shit out of them, and the crop is ruined. The farmer now has less than dick. The landowner shows up and says, 'Where's my five grand?' The farmer says, 'Hey, the crop was, uh, ruined, no fault of my own.' Landowner says, 'I don't give a shit, you owe me, and you've got *x* amount of time to come up with it.' Extortion 101."

Ryan put a finger to his chin, considering. This was what was called *second-order effects*; the unintended, farther-reaching results of kinetic action. It was the kind of thing he generally thought of as not his problem. "I feel for the farmer," said Ryan, "but isn't heroin already pretty high on this country's list of problems?"

"It is," said Pete. "It is. But here's part one of the kicker. Haji got into the provincial records office the other day. Did some research on the village. Most of the fields outside of the village are owned by Bashir Daoud Khan."

Ryan leaned back. "Bashir Daoud Khan—*the* Khan—that everyone's always talking about? The politician?"

"Correct."

"Isn't he the Afghan version of Tony Soprano?"

"He is," said Pete. "But without the therapist."

"We Afghans are not very big on therapy," said the cleaner.

"Okay," said Ryan. "But from what I've heard, Khan is *our* Tony Soprano, right?"

A funny look passed over Pete's face— half-chagrined, half-amused. He picked up his water bottle from the table and downed it all. Then he took out his cigarettes. He offered his pack to Ryan and the cleaner, who both declined. Lighting up, Pete said, "Let me tell you about Bashir Daoud Khan, our very own Tony Soprano."

Ryan listened. Pete and the cleaner, fluidly taking over the narrative from one another, told him what they knew. There was history between the Ghost and Bashir Daoud Khan. Bad history. After the cleaner had turned up the records on Haji Baba, he'd turned to his seemingly endless network of uncles in Kandahar City and put some questions to them. Careful questions, of course, steeped in the intricacies of respect and discretion. Nevertheless, it had taken him only half a day to put the history together, and what he brought to Pete was astonishing.

According to the uncles, **Khan had** been born around 1965 on a farm near **Shah Wali Khot**. His family were poor, but in **1984 their** farm and what little they had were destroyed in a Russian sweep operation. They fled to Peshawar, where they had extended family. Not long after that, young Bashir joined the Hezb-i Islami Khalis mujahedeen group, attracted by their power and popularity in Pesh. He was then sent as a fighter back to Kandahar, where for some time he was undistinguished.

After a year or two, the uncles said, Khan had arranged to be transferred to the militia led by the Ghost. Even at that time the Ghost's reputation was as far-reaching as it was fearsome; the young Khan, looking to increase his own reputation, was drawn by this. During the Battle of Arghandab in 1987, Khan assisted in bringing down a Russian plane. The pilot survived the crash and was captured by the mujahedeen. In an effort to show his strength to the Ghost and his comrades alike,

Khan tortured the pilot. Not just tortured him, it was said; Khan raped and debased the pilot repeatedly. Made the man less than a dancing boy, less than a dog. This incident was related by the uncles to the cleaner (and in turn to Pete) with various measures of indifference and horror, and with various differences in the minor details, but all the uncles agreed that it had indeed happened.

In any case, the rape and torture did not impress the Ghost the way Khan intended. The Ghost said the incident showed a lack of discipline and morality. Worse than that, it showed *pride* on the part of the young man. Utterly disgraced, Khan was sent back to Peshawar, while the Ghost and the other front-line mujahedeen continued to fight the Soviets for another two years.

The HIK *shura* decided to retain young Bashir Daoud Khan; despite his brash taste for violence, he was smart and devoted. But as if to reinforce his disgraceful dismissal from the Ghost's forward unit, he was given a lowly logistics job, inventorying the network's livestock, vehicles, fuel, and medical supplies in their hideouts on the other side of the Khyber Pass.

As luck would have it, however, it was in logistics that Khan truly excelled, bringing the network to levels of organization they'd never achieved before. As the eighties came to a close, the *shura* gave Khan more and more responsibility. By the time the Soviets pulled out in 1989, Khan had become the unofficial chief of HIK's logistics and finances—a role in which he built strong relations with Pakistani intelligence, other mujahedeen groups across Afghanistan, and, most importantly, the American CIA.

Meanwhile, with the war against the Soviets over, the Ghost did what ghosts do—he vanished.

"You've been doing some research," said Ryan.

"I have."

"And let me guess—you'd be in serious shit if your boss knew *what* you were researching."

Pete tried, and failed, to blow a smoke ring. "Absolutely."

Ryan drummed his fingers on the tabletop. The sunlight was starting to encroach on the little patch of shade they'd found, and with the sunlight came the heat and the sweat. Pete was watching him intently, expectantly. The cleaner was smiling.

"What do you want, Pete?"

"It's an overwatch task."

"First time, when we went down to the village, it was just me you needed," said Ryan. "Second time was the city, and we know how that went. But now, if you're talking about an actual overwatch task, you're talking about my guys."

"There's no asset like you," said Pete.

Anger flashed through Ryan. He felt hot blood come into his face. He took a breath and held it until the anger subsided. Then, carefully, he said, "Look, get Khan added to the high value target list. Then we can put a fifty-cal round through him. That's our job. Until then, I don't know why I should get my snipers involved in this, Pete. And to be honest, by the sounds of it, maybe you should take a step back yourself—before you fuck up your own career." Ryan stood up from the picnic table. He finished his water, crumpled up the empty bottle and tossed it into a garbage drum a metre away. "I've gotta get back to work."

"Hold on," said Pete. "Haji, tell him what else you found out. Tell him who the farmer is."

"The farmer's name is Abdul Malik," said the cleaner.

"Abdul Malik," said Ryan. "This is the guy who

owes Khan five grand? What do I care what his name is?"

"And Abdul Malik's father is Haji Malik," said Pete. "The Lion of the Desert. The *Ghost*, Ryan."

**- - -**

Until now—until Pete and the cleaner had started overturning stones—there had been no answers as to why the Ghost had reappeared. The total picture was not complete; not even the cleaner's many uncles knew exactly what was supposed to happen between the Ghost and Khan. But without question, it was a matter of Pashtunwali. That could not be underestimated.

"But if we could get him to work with *us*," said Pete.

"Why?" said Ryan. "Why does having the Ghost on our side matter?"

"You said it yourself, and you're not the only one who's said it: Khan is a fucking gangster. He might be too well connected to take out, but we're making some pretty deep ethical compromises by sleeping with him, you know? But the Ghost, he's a true warrior. He's a man of honour."

A light had come into Pete's eyes. A not-quite-sane light. He looked almost like a fire-and-brimstone preacher.

Ryan had returned to the picnic table. It was still only midmorning, and yet it felt like a huge, irrevocable span of time had gone by.

"You want to trade Khan for the Ghost," said Ryan.

"*Yes*," said Pete. "Forget roads, Ryan. If we make an ally out of someone like the Lion of the Desert, that's a *real* Alexandria."

The reference meant nothing to Ryan, but he wasn't giving it any thought. Gone native, gone crazy, fire-and-brimstone preacher or not, there was something to what Pete was saying. Ryan could not help but realize the hook was set once again. He leaned back against the top of the picnic table for a long time. He looked at his hands. His trigger finger. He said, "So where does Six-Six fit in?"

"We think Abdul Malik's payment date is close," said Pete. "Three days away at most."

"The Ghost is still inside the city," said the cleaner. "My uncles believe he is gathering together the money from all his old friends."

"But he wouldn't take the money you offered him," said Ryan.

"Well, he said it best," said Pete. "Only a fool receives a gift without knowing what for. Anyway, what we need from you are eyes and ears on that village. Comings and goings, who's there, why. Ongoing overwatch. This is how your war and mine come together, Ryan."

"I got my dets spread all over the company's AO. But I guess I could redeploy them, rotate them on a two-days-on, two-days-off kind of thing. Starting tonight."

"That should do it," said Pete.

"But their job is overwatch, right? I don't want them getting mixed up in something like what happened to me in Kandahar City."

"It's their eyes I need," said Pete. "Nothing else. Not yet, anyway."

Ryan nodded. "We'll have to get the chain of command to buy in to this."

"That part is the easiest," said Pete. "This is all just a preliminary recce for Op Open Highway. I'm gathering data and atmospherics on the area around Hyena Road. That's all anybody needs to know."

"You're your own worst enemy, aren't you," said Ryan.

Pete just laughed.

- - -

Jenn watched as Ryan and Pete Mitchell and a local man chatted with each other around a picnic table in the common area. She'd almost run into the three men—almost—on her way back to the CP from the medical station. Only at the last second had she spotted them. Before they'd seen her, she'd ducked into a porta-potty on the far side of the ball hockey rink. She sat on the toilet seat, half dizzy with the latrine's stifling heat and rancid air. She held the door open a crack so she could watch the men. She was desperately willing them to finish up their conversation and part ways. Only then could she cover the rest of the distance to the CP—without running into Ryan.

Jenn's heart was pounding. Nothing in the world felt quite real. Half an hour ago she'd been inside the Sperwan Ghar medical station. The interior of the medical station was as utilitarian as everything else, all canvas and plywood and stainless steel.

Two of the medical-tech NCOs had gotten Jenn propped up on an exam table. Then the medical officer, Captain Heather Cooke, had taken over, pulling a privacy curtain shut. Jenn was grateful for what little discretion they could manage.

She and Heather made small talk for a little while. Then, before long, Heather had Jenn pull her shirt up to the bottom of her bra and squeezed some cool gel onto Jenn's belly. She rolled a plastic transducer over the still taut skin.

"If we find something, what do we do?" said Heather. "You know I'm supposed to report it."

"I . . . Well, I'm asking you not to," said Jenn.

Heather nodded. "How long has it been?"

"About eight weeks. I thought maybe I'd just skipped a period."

"That can certainly happen, of course. Stress and whatnot. Especially if you're filling in for the company OC."

Heather adjusted the transducer and looked at the monitor beside the exam table. Jenn considered Heather a friend, but it occurred to her that they weren't very close. They really weren't more than amicable colleagues. Heather had her set of orders to abide by, and if she found—

"Oh my," said Heather.

The medical officer rotated the monitor so Jenn could see what was on it. There was a tiny black form in the midst of a grey sea. Jenn felt the world drop away from beneath her. She leaned her head back on the exam table. She opened her mouth and closed it again. In one instant, her entire life had changed.

And now Jenn was sitting in the porta-potty, watching the men at the picnic table like a spy. Heather had promised not to report the situation, but she did say that Jenn would have to report it to the chain of command at some point, and sooner would be better than later. There wasn't any feasible way to hide the changes her body would soon start to undergo.

At last the little meeting at the picnic table broke up. Pete and the Afghan man walked off in one direction; Ryan headed off a different way. Jenn blew out a ragged sigh of relief. Heather was right—Jenn would not be able to hide this for very long. But she simply could not face Ryan. Not yet.

# 9

Six-Six, still under Travis's command, departed from Sperwan Ghar at twenty-three hundred hours that night. Ryan, despite how much he wanted to be out there with them, was going to stay back and work in the CP. The snipers' mission parameters hadn't really changed—it was still an observe-and-report task—but the location had been changed from Hyena Road to Haji Baba. At suppertime, Travis had first received a one-on-one briefing from Ryan. The briefing had included some photocopied pictures of a couple of VIPs. Half an hour later, Travis had given updated orders to the det. None of the other snipers had any questions; a change in scenery from Hyena might actually be refreshing, even if it was the village where they'd nearly been overrun not long ago.

The det's departure from Sper was initially via a LAV patrol. The patrol went four kilometres west on Hyena Road, ever deeper into the Horn of Panjwayi. At the four-kilometre mark, Six-Six debussed from the LAVs and moved into the grape fields and dry creek beds south of the road. There was no moon, but the stars were bright and abundant.

It took Six-Six four hours to move three kilometres cross-country. They halted often, silently taking stock of their surroundings, checking their bearings. Insurgents and IEDs notwithstanding, there were still plenty of Soviet mines and ordnance out here in the fields, just waiting to be stepped on. The terrain itself was hazardous as well; a Canadian officer had died a year or two before simply by falling into an unmarked cistern and drowning in the brackish water at the bottom.

By zero-three-thirty, the snipers had made it to a small crag that Travis had identified on his map before they'd departed. The crag reared up from the fields beside an unnamed dirt road. Four hundred metres to the southeast lay Haji Baba. Some lonesome lanterns flickered here and there, but otherwise the village was dark. There was no sound save the wind.

The snipers were thirty minutes ascending the crag, another thirty minutes establishing their hide in a shallow fissure just below the summit. By that time the very first edges of false dawn were creeping into the eastern sky. Wilf and Hickey were catching some sleep under their blankets. Tank was on the spotter's scope. Travis was on the Tac-50.

Just then, something made a commotion on the dirt road below. The night air carried the sounds clearly—frantic scrabbling and digging. Without making any noise of their own, Tank and Travis trained their optics down the hill.

What came into sight, eerie through the night vision, was a lone hyena by the side of the road. Matted fur and stark ribs. The hyena was pawing at the carcass of a long-dead sheep.

- - -

The long rays of dawn brought thin silver mist up from the ground. The day's heat would soon descend. Magnified through the scopes, Haji

Baba slowly woke up. It started with the call to prayer coming from the village's solitary concrete mosque. The mosque had no minaret—only a beat-up loudspeaker affixed to the top of the little dome. After the prayers had finished, a small number of farmers made their way out into the surrounding fields. A boy shepherded some goats down one of the narrow laneways. A burqa-clad woman held a plastic bucket under the hand pump in the village square. From their position, Six-Six had a particularly good view, almost dead-on, of the Malik compound at the edge of the square. The blasted wall was still unrepaired. A single lantern—no brighter than a spark at that distance—sputtered in one of the compound's windows.

Travis thumbed his comms. "Three, this is Six-Six Delta. Sitrep. The village is starting its day. Normal pattern of life at this time. Over."

The voice of one of the signallers came back. "Three, acknowledged."

Beside Travis, Tank was taking long blinks and rubbing the bridge of his nose.

"Go grab some rack," said Travis. "Send the kid over."

"I don't know how you keep going, Trav," Tank muttered. "You're a goddamn robot."

Tank crawled out from under the camouflage netting that they'd draped over the Tac-50 and the spotter's scope. Travis kept observation on the village. Ten minutes later, Wilf scuttled in beside him. The kid looked groggy. Thin stubble had come out on his jaw and chin.

"Morning, bud," said Travis. "You're on the scope. Stay awake or I'll push you down the hill."

Wilf nodded. He worked himself into a sitting position behind the spotter's scope, adjusted the reticle, and began to observe. Travis leaned back from the Tac-50 and took an IMP pouch—beef ravioli, could be much worse—out of his vest and cut it open with his knife. It would've been better heated up, but he was hungry. As he ate, he leaned forward to peek over the forward edge of their little hide, down the slope to the dirt road. The hyena they'd seen before daybreak was gone.

"Vehicle approaching," Wilf whispered.

Travis set his meal down and looked through the Tac-50. A small hatchback was coming into Haji Baba along the "main" north-south route— the gravel access that connected the village with

Hyena Road. A small plume of dust rose behind the car.

At the same time, two figures emerged from the Malik compound. One was the young guy; Travis had learned his name was Abdul. The other, taller and leaner, was the old man himself. The Ghost, Ryan had called him. The Ghost who'd given them protection. The two men stood in the compound's small courtyard, facing each other. The hatchback came to a stop outside the ruined wall. Father and son embraced. Then the Ghost walked out to the car and got in the passenger seat. A moment later, the car had turned around and driven back the way it had come. Abdul stood outside the house, watching the car as it disappeared. Then he went inside.

"What was all that?" said Wilf. "Was that important?"

Travis did not answer. Instead he sent the description of what they'd observed up the net.

After a slight delay, Captain Bowman's voice came back: "Six-Six Delta, Three Niner Alpha. Acknowledged."

And no sooner had Captain Bowman finished transmitting her message than another voice, male, came through Travis's headset: "Six-Six Delta, this is Golf Niner Whiskey. Really good information, thanks for that. Keep it up. Out."

Travis smiled thinly. Golf Niner Whiskey. That had to be Ryan's new friend, the batshit crazy captain from KAF. Apparently wherever Captain Golf Niner Whiskey went, a whole lot of trouble followed.

■ ■ ■

Ryan knew Jenn well enough to plainly notice the dangerous shadow that had crossed her face when Pete had transmitted over the Charlie Company net. *Really good information, thanks for that. Keep it up.* The overwatch on Haji Baba might have been Pete's plan, but the CP was squarely Jenn's domain. She didn't say anything, but she did give Ryan a brief get-a-grip-on-this-guy look.

Ryan and Pete had come into the CP at dawn. Despite his best intentions to stay cool, Ryan couldn't deny that he was eager to know what was happening out at Haji Baba. He desperately wanted to be out there with the det, *his* det, but he understood that he needed to be back here, acting as the go-between.

At least Ryan had the good sense to linger a few paces away from Jenn's battle board. Pete was hunched over the map, wearing a headset he'd taken from one of the signallers. The CP crew—the sergeant and the three or four junior NCOs—were giving the peculiar captain some grudging, silent space, but Jenn wouldn't last long, especially if Pete jumped on the net again.

Ten minutes passed and nothing happened. The last sitrep from Six-Six had been the Ghost departing in a car. Ryan had no idea where he was going. Back to Kandahar City, maybe, to keep trying to raise the money his son owed Khan? The cleaner might know, but he'd left after supper the day before. Pete was staying tight-lipped and pensive.

At seven hundred hours, other sitreps started to come in. One of the platoons was on a security patrol outside Sper; they had nothing to report so far, but they were remaining vigilant. A logistics convoy reported that they were stopped on Hyena Road, half a klick away, checking out a suspicious culvert . . .

"Jenn, let's check in with Six-Six again," said Pete. "I want to know if anything's changed."

The dangerous shadow crossed Jenn's face again. Pete did not seem to notice. Jenn seemed about to say something, so Ryan quickly stepped over to the battle board. "Hey, Captain Mitchell, let's go get some breakfast before the kitchen stops serving."

"I'm fine," said Pete. "I want to stick it out here in case—"

"They'll call in if they've got something," said Ryan. He turned to one of the signallers. "Hey bud, we're gonna be in the mess or maybe just outside of it. If Six-Six sends in anything, *anything*, come grab us, will you?"

The signaller nodded that he would. Pete reluctantly took his borrowed headset off and set it down on the battle board. Ryan walked with him over to the CP door and half-pushed him through it. Jenn followed a step behind.

"Thank you," she said quietly.

"I know how you work," said Ryan.

A faint smile touched her lips and lightened her eyes.

"Hey, I heard you were in the med station

yesterday," said Ryan, his voice barely more than a whisper. "Is everything okay?"

She looked away from him. "Everything's fine. Just a checkup. Go get breakfast. I'll send for you if anything goes down."

---

As soon as they were away from the CP, Pete seemed to unwind a little. Ryan led the way through the line in the kitchen. They both filled their plates with scrambled eggs and bacon. They got some coffee and sat down at a table in the mess tent. It was the same table where Ryan had had breakfast with Travis and the others only the day before. How quickly things changed.

"Why do you think the Ghost went back to KC?" said Ryan. "More, uh, fundraising?"

Pete nodded. "Probably. Other than his son and his granddaughters, and unless Khan happens to show up, there's nothing much for the Ghost in Haji Baba."

"Do you think Khan *would* show up?"

"It's hard to say," said Pete. "On the one hand, Khan has spent a long time learning how to work on things from a distance. He's smart, like the *best* gangsters. In that case I doubt you'd ever see him within a hundred miles of Haji Baba, not when he's got people to do the dirty stuff for him. On the other hand he's vain, like *most* gangsters. When he fucked up that Russian pilot, way back in the eighties, that was vanity. That was him putting his face on something big and bad, you know? If he's done something like that before, he might do it again . . . But now? I really don't know. Your guys might spend the next thirty-six hours staring at rocks."

"That would be fine," said Ryan, lifting a forkful of eggs into his mouth. "We've had a lot of engagements on Hyena over the last couple months. Staring at rocks might do the guys some good."

"You've taken a lot of guys down on Hyena?"

"Yeah," said Ryan. "They keep coming, though."

They ate in silence for a minute or two. The silence was even kind of companionable. Pete was still a maniac, Ryan thought, but at least he had finally given Ryan some understanding of the chess-game war he was fighting.

Pete scraped up the last of his breakfast and

swallowed it. Instead of suggesting they go back to the CP—as Ryan guessed he would—Pete said, "What was it like, your first time?"

The question was forthright. Ryan found Pete looking at him with genuine interest. He knew exactly what Pete was asking, but for a moment at least he sidestepped. "You mean," said Ryan, "you and your wife have never . . . ?"

Pete grinned. "No. Never."

They both laughed.

"You never shot anyone directly?" said Ryan.

"Me? No. Well, I don't know but probably not. Even the other day in KC. I put a lot of rounds downrange, but I have no idea if I hit anybody."

Ryan nodded, patting his mouth with a paper napkin. It wasn't common in a gunfight to actually see if you were shooting somebody. The rounds flew back and forth and sometimes people got hit, but it was nothing like the movies. Sniping, on the other hand . . .

For some reason, he found himself opening up. Maybe it was the straight, genuinely interested way he'd been asked. He said, "First time's a bit weird. Way back on my first tour, I was lined up on this bad guy at about 750 metres. No wind. And I can put four rounds one on top of the other at that distance. Mentally I was fine. But my body went nuts. My heart was pounding but, like, really hard and my eyes went all foggy and I got this kind of tremor in my trigger arm. So I got off the scope, went through a mental checklist, calmed things down. Got back on the rifle. And . . . I was fine after that."

"You engaged," said Pete.

"Oh, yeah," said Ryan. "I lit him up."

Pete seemed to consider this for a moment. Then he said, "You know, a lot of guys—and it's like a big percentage—never engage another human being with direct fire. It's not that they can't—it's more like something inside them makes them shoot high or off or whatever. What do you think that's all about?"

"Training. Or maybe something more. I don't know. I never had a problem after that first one."

"Me neither."

"I thought you said you never shot anyone," said Ryan.

"I did say that," said Pete. "But people have died on my account, of that I have no doubt at all. For you it's direct fire with a rifle. For me it's getting certain people to meet, to talk to each other—"

"Warrant Murphy? Sorry to interrupt."

Ryan and Pete glanced over. The signaller from the CP was standing at the end of the table.

"Your guys are calling in a contact, Warrant," said the signaller. "Captain Bowman says you and the captain here should come on back to the CP."

---

Three white Toyota Sequoia SUVs were charging down the gravel road into Haji Baba. By the time the vehicles pulled into the square, the village had suddenly—almost spontaneously—closed itself up, the same way it had when Six-Six had first entered it in the middle of their shootout. The windows were all closed, the shops were shuttered, nobody remained in sight. The pattern of life was all wrong.

Travis and Wilf observed from the crag.

Travis thumbed his comms. "Three Niner Alpha, this is Six-Six Delta. We are observing three times up-armoured white SUVs. They've come into the village square. They're right outside the objective compound. All pattern of life has, uh, disappeared."

Captain Bowman's voice came back: "Six-Six Delta, Three Niner Alpha, I acknowledge your last. Keep the sitreps coming."

Two whole minutes went by. The SUVs continued to idle outside the Malik compound. Nothing else moved.

"What's going on?" Wilf whispered.

"I don't know," said Travis. "Go wake up Tank and Hickey. As of now we're standing to."

Wilf crawled out from under the cam net. Travis could hear him shaking the other two snipers awake, trying to stay as quiet as possible. Travis kept watch on the village through his scope.

Another minute, and then the doors of each SUV opened up and half a dozen men piled out. Of the six men, four were dressed almost identically—black garments, black turbans, mismatched tactical gear. But it was the remaining two men, one young and the other older, neither of them dressed like their escort, who stood out the most.

■ ■ ■

Pete and Ryan were back in the company CP, listening to the reports from Six-Six. Pete had no need to borrow a headset this time; the signallers had turned the speakers on and everything was loud and clear. Jenn was standing rigidly beside the battle board, her arms crossed, her brow deeply furrowed. Pete started to approach the battle board, but a hand on his arm lightly restrained him. He looked. Ryan was shaking his head. Then Ryan gestured with his chin at Jenn, as if to say, *Stay out of her way*. Pete felt a flash of irritation, but he nodded and stayed put.

The voice of the acting sniper det commander—Ryan said the guy's name was Travis—cracked over the speakers: "Four times Taliban have gotten out of the vehicles."

"Six-Six Delta, Three Niner Alpha," said Jenn. "Can you confirm, four times Taliban?"

"Six-Six Delta, yes," said Travis. "Black turbans, black outfits, god-awful beards."

"Three Niner Alpha, roger. Are they armed?"

"Six-Six Delta, negative. I am not observing any weapons at this time."

Taliban right out there in the open, Pete thought. They're not trying to hide who they are. This is a statement.

At that moment, Travis's sitrep continued

from the speakers: "I've also got two times men who are dressed more like civilians. The first is in his forties, I'd say. He's got thinning hair and a short beard. He is short but he has a big gut. The other is younger . . ."

Pete breathed in and held it and let it out slowly. He turned to Ryan. "Did you give your guys those pictures I gave you last night?"

Ryan started to nod, but almost immediately, Travis was speaking again: "Based on our imagery, I assess that the older person is—let me check the initials here, wait one—Bravo Delta Kilo. The younger person is . . . Hotel Whiskey Kilo."

Bravo Delta Kilo, Bashir Daoud Khan. Hotel Whiskey Kilo, Hamid Wali Khan. Pete closed his eyes.

Jenn had the same photocopied pictures Six-Six had been given before they'd deployed. She'd pinned them on the corner of the battle board. Pete could hear her asking the snipers to confirm the VIPs. "Confirmed," came the reply. And in his mind, Pete heard his own words coming back to him from only half an hour ago: *That was him putting his face on something big and bad, you know? Your guys might spend the next thirty-six hours staring at rocks.*

Pete opened his eyes. Jenn and Ryan were both staring at him.

"You didn't think your VIPs would actually show up out there, did you?" said Jenn.

"I—no," said Pete. "Not this fast, anyway. Christ. They must have passed the Ghost on Hyena Road."

Jenn nodded and gave Pete a tight-lipped *now what?* expression. Pete picked up the headset he'd removed before breakfast. Neither Jenn nor Ryan tried to stop him. Pete pressed the switch. "Six-Six Delta, this is Golf Niner Whiskey. Can you confirm nobody, including the two VIPs, are carrying weapons?"

The sniper's voice came back immediately: "Confirmed."

"Roger," said Pete. "What are they doing now?"

There was a delay, five or six seconds, before Travis replied, "Currently both VIPs and one Taliban escort are standing in front of the objective compound. I have no audio on them, but call sign Bravo Delta Kilo looks like he's yelling. He's got his fist in the air—wait, someone's coming outside."

. . .

Through the Tac-50 scope, Travis watched as Abdul Malik emerged from the house and stood in the little courtyard, three metres away from the elder and younger Khan and their Taliban escort. Around them, the rest of Haji Baba remained conspicuously lifeless.

Wilf was back beside Travis, watching through the spotter's scope, already quietly listing the wind gusts and deflection. Outside the cam net, Tank and Hickey were wide awake and in position, maintaining their local security. The sun overhead was in its midmorning position and the heat was building.

Travis watched and waited. Thus far none of the four Taliban showed any weapons, but Travis knew they had them. Pistols under their vests, perhaps, or AKs stacked up in their SUVs. All Travis needed was to *see* the enemy weapons . . .

He had already chambered a round in the Tac-50. His finger was itching to lever the safety off.

Down in the courtyard, Bashir Khan was now standing right in front of Abdul. Abdul was holding his hands out, palms forward. It was a candid gesture of pleading, even over the intervening distance. The Talib who'd come with Khan into the courtyard shouldered past Abdul and disappeared inside the house. Khan seemed to speak for a minute more, then took a step back, shaking his head. Instantly Hamid Khan came forward and slapped Abdul across the face. Abdul took the blow with a lowered head.

"Holy shit," said Wilf.

Travis thumbed his comms. "Six-Six Delta. I have hostile action against civilians."

"Six-Six Delta, this is Golf Niner Whiskey. Clarify hostile action."

"An assault," said Travis. "Call sign Hotel Whiskey Kilo just smacked call sign Alpha Mike across the face." He released the PTT switch.

"Holy *shit*," said Wilf.

Travis looked. The Talib had emerged from the house. He was walking back across the courtyard, and on either side of him were Abdul's little daughters. The Talib was dragging them by the hair. Abdul dropped to his knees. His mouth hung open in a wide, soundless cry.

- - -

For a full minute, there was no sound in the CP. The signallers and the duty sergeant were staring hard at their logbooks. Ryan had gone pale and livid colour had come into Jenn's face. Pete planted his knuckles on the battle board and leaned forward. From this perspective, Haji Baba was just a tiny marking on the big provincial map, and yet it somehow seemed to be swelling up from the paper.

Travis's voice came over the speakers, cutting the silence like a thunderclap, repeating what he'd just reported: "This is Six-Six Delta. I say again, *they are dragging young children out of the house.* Over."

Jenn blinked. She pushed her switch. "Six-Six Delta, this is Three Niner Alpha, I acknowledge. Do you have imminent threat?"

A long, awful pause, and then Travis came back: "Six-Six Delta, negative. Still no weapons visible on anybody. But they're dragging these girls to the trucks. Authorize to engage. I'm getting ready to take the shot."

Jenn started to push her switch.

"Jenn," said Pete, "this is my op. I'm stepping in." She looked at him for a long moment. Then she looked down at the map. The nod of her head was barely perceptible, but it was there. Pete pushed his own switch. "Six-Six Delta, this is Golf Niner Whiskey. Negative. Sit tight. Over."

"What in the fuck?" Ryan hissed. "Take them down!"

Pete stared hard at the map, as if he could set fire to it with his eyes. *It'd be a fuck of a lot easier to do what we came here to do if Khan stopped breathing for some reason . . . If only . . .*

Yes. But it could not go like this. There was far too much at stake. For the first time, Pete clearly saw the size of the house of cards standing on Bashir Daoud Khan's shoulders. To Ryan and Jenn he said, "Unless they pull weapons, we can't get involved."

The speakers crackled again: "Six-Six Delta. For God's sake. We can intervene! Request authority. Over." Even over the radio there was an audible edge in Travis's voice.

"Golf Niner Whiskey, negative," said Pete. "Unless you see a weapon, do not intervene."

The weighted silence prevailed throughout the CP for another several minutes. When Travis finally came back, his voice sounded utterly flat: "This is Six-Six Delta. Sitrep. Four times Taliban and two times VIPs have departed. With the two kids. Call sign Alpha Mike is, well, he's just sitting there outside his house. Pattern of life in the village is coming back to normal. Sitrep ends. Out."

"Jesus fucking Christ," said Ryan.

"Settle down, Warrant Murphy," said Jenn.

Ryan looked at her. His mouth moved, as if he might say something. Then he turned around and walked out of the CP.

— — —

The day's heat had become relentless. The sun was too bright. For a long time Travis remained as he was, poised behind the Tac-50, watching through the scope. Beside him, Wilf stayed silent. Four hundred metres away, the dust that the SUVs had kicked up on their departure was still hanging in the air. Abdul Malik was on his knees, unmoving, in the courtyard outside his house. In that posture he looked a little bit like the lone bomber Six-Six had engaged on Hyena Road the week before.

— — —

"You were way out of line," said Jenn.

She'd followed Ryan outside. The two of them were standing in a patch of hard sunlight ten paces away from the CP's entrance.

Ryan could barely assemble a coherent thought. He was sweating all over, and he could hear his pulse thundering in his ears. He felt like none of this was real. It couldn't be. "Why didn't you override?"

"Because this was an effects reconnaissance and it's their call and it's the rules of engagement and you know that."

"It's *children.*"

She visibly recoiled at that, looked away. She seemed to gather herself, and after a long beat she said, "You and I need to talk."

Over Jenn's shoulder, Ryan saw Pete come out of the CP. Pete did not look at them. He started walking away—God knew where he thought he was going—pawing at his pockets for his cigarettes.

"No, we don't need to talk," said Ryan. "We're good."

"Ryan," said Jenn. "There's something you need to—"

Ryan broke away from her and went in Pete's direction. He didn't know if she'd follow him or not. He didn't care. His palms were wet. He clenched his fists and unclenched them and clenched them again. "Hey! Mitchell! What are those girls, like, eight, ten years old? And we just stand there? What's going to happen to them now?"

A couple of junior NCOs, ambling in the direction of the gym, started to intersect Ryan's path. Then they saw him and stopped short. He stormed past them.

"*Mitchell!*"

Pete stopped beside a row of plastic latrines. He'd got his cigarettes out and had lit one. Ryan caught up with him. Keeping his back turned, Pete said, "The girls will be sold. Khan will turn them over to his network, who will put them on the market. Whatever they get above five grand they keep . . . but Khan gets his five grand. And the girls will end up in some shitty marriage in Dubai or, worse, sucking dick in a brothel outside Okotoks."

"You know this and we don't intervene?"

"We didn't intervene because we didn't have

imminent threat. That's the rules of engagement and I had to make that call. And we didn't intervene because Khan is covered by a roof on top of which is a big fucking sign that reads CIA. He's *our* gangster, remember? So, if you want to fuck up our presence here, if you want to personally destroy General Rilmen, then be my guest and shoot him."

Ryan took a deep breath of the hot, stinking air. His rage was subsiding, and in its wake was exhaustion. "I thought you said this is where your war and mine come together."

Pete turned around to face him. "It wasn't supposed to go down like that. I did not think that was the game Khan would play ... at least not yet."

"This fucking Khan asshole isn't playing a game here," said Ryan. "Neither am I or my guys. *Nobody's* here to play games."

"No, and we're not here so kids can fly kites, either."

"Then what the fuck are we doing here?"

"We're rolling back the clock," said Pete. "We're stacking the deck so this time the crazies don't win." Abruptly, Pete looked at his half-smoked cigarette, as if seeing it for the first time.

He pitched it on the ground and rubbed it out with his boot. "Listen, Ryan, don't think I don't feel for those girls, 'cause I do. And we'll try and find them. But right now, in the bigger picture, bringing the Ghost onto our side is the only thing that matters."

"And how in the hell do you think you'll even interest him? Your money didn't work, so what?"

"*Badal*," said Pete, quietly, almost to himself. "The Ghost will have to make *badal*." Pete looked at Ryan. "*Badal* is—"

"I know what it is," Ryan spat. "It's revenge. You know what else I know? You can take your secret war and your *badal* and your Pashtunwali and shove it up your ass, Captain Mitchell. This, all of this, is on you. Charge me for insubordination if you want, *sir*, but unless you figure out how to make this right, then you stay the fuck away from me and my guys."

Pete said nothing.

- - -

Pete said nothing. He watched as Ryan turned around and stormed away. Ryan did not return to the CP; he angled off into a nearby weather haven and slammed the door behind him. Pete stood by the latrines for another minute. He was craving another cigarette, but for some reason the idea of smoking nauseated him. Many things nauseated him in that moment—least of all the smell of the latrines, most of all himself. He took out his cellphone and called the cleaner.

"Haji? It's Pete . . . Yes, I'm still at Sperwan Ghar, but I'm going to go back to KAF ASAP . . . Anyhow there are things you'll hear soon if your uncles haven't already told you. Something Khan has done. It's going to cause problems for everybody."

# 10

FOLLOWING HIS MIDDAY PRAYERS, the old man returned to the tiny rooms he'd been borrowing at the back of Ghulam's bakery. The day was very hot and the city seemed more foreign to him than ever. There was nothing about it that seemed to hearken back to his youth anymore. The house where he'd grown up, along with his father and uncles' business, had been no more than a kilometre from the bakery, but all that stood there now was a sheet-metal-sided warehouse of some kind. Even the orchard had been paved over. He recognized none of it.

No matter, he told himself. This was just the useless, melancholy reminiscing of an old man. An old man who needed a nap.

As he opened the door to his room, Ghulam appeared at the other end of the narrow corridor, where it angled off to the storefront. "Can I bring you anything, Haji Malik? Some naan and honey? Some tea?"

The old man smiled. "No, my friend. I think I'll just lie down for a little while. I have more old friends to call on this evening."

Ghulam nodded affably and disappeared in the direction of the storefront. The old man went into his room and softly closed the door behind him. The room was dim and relatively cool. He reclined on some cushions on the floor and folded his hands on his stomach.

Ghulam's father had fought in the old man's *tanzim* in the old days. Ghulam the elder was two or three years dead now, but his son—although a self-effacing baker—was still fiercely loyal to him, and by extension to his father's legendary former commander. When the old man had returned to Kandahar to settle his own son's account, Ghulam the younger had been the very first to offer—no, to *insist*—on providing him a place to stay inside the city.

Not that staying at the bakery went completely unnoticed, of course. He wanted to be a ghost these days far more than he wanted to be a lion, but word had still somehow gotten out. There'd been that eager ISAF officer who'd come to palaver with the old man, the same day the city was attacked. The ISAF officer had brought with him the same young soldier to whom the old man had given *panah*, back in Haji Baba, some days before that. There was a surprising understanding of Pashtunwali in the ISAF officer's voice, and a cunning in his eyes, but the old man had seen *true* fire in the younger soldier's eyes. That soldier was the kind who might have stood tall with the mujahedeen at Sangsar, in the Arghandab, in Maywand, in countless other battles in those long-gone years.

In any case, if ISAF had been able to track the old man down to Ghulam's bakery, then surely others knew of his return as well. Khan, for example. As the old man knew, Khan had eyes and ears all over the city. All over the province. As a young man, Khan's prideful barbarism had been astonishing; to this day the old man was still sickened by the horror that had been inflicted on that nameless, long-dead helicopter pilot, even if he was a Soviet. He didn't know if Khan still had those kinds of penchants, although he suspected he did. But the old man also knew that Khan was a savvy businessman—perhaps even more than he was anything else—and it was as a business-man that the old man intended to settle Abdul's account with him. No blood needed to be shed now, not over some wretched patch of opium.

Sooner or later, the old man mused, Khan would run afoul of ISAF or the Pakistani spies or the Taliban or all three, and he would be dealt with accordingly. By that time, the old man would be far away from here, nearing the end of his own life with as clean a conscience as he could ever hope for.

Inshallah.

He dozed. The orchard of his boyhood home came to him. There were wrens flitting from tree to tree, and there were ripe pomegranates hanging from the branches. You could pluck them and break them open and the seeds inside were as big as the end of your thumb. Delicious beyond words. The old man saw his father and mother in the orchard. He saw his only son. And he saw his granddaughters on the narrow path, leading him by the hand, running ahead, turning back to see if he still followed. Laughing as the wrens sang, with hearts too big for their tiny bodies . . .

The knocking on his door woke him up with a start. He didn't know how long he'd been dozing. A lifetime, it felt like, but it couldn't have been more than minutes. The orchard was fading from his mind, paved over into the nothingness it was today. He stood up slowly. The old pain in his leg was at its worst whenever he woke from a nap. He shuffled to the door and opened it.

On the threshold stood Ghulam. He was grim and pale. Right away the old man knew something was badly wrong.

"There's word from Haji Baba," said Ghulam.

The old man nodded. As the baker told him what had happened that morning, the old man simply listened, saying nothing. He felt simultaneously removed from the world and anchored to it. Something stirred inside his heart—a feeling he'd almost forgotten altogether.

The Lion was rising.

**11**

No word about the latest incident
in Haji Baba had made it to any of the higher
headquarters or intelligence circles on KAF, at
least not as far as Pete could tell. A day after his
return from Sperwan Ghar, he had supper in the
DFAC with Chewey. She did not indicate that
she'd heard anything about Khan and his Taliban
pals kidnapping some young girls. Pete kept the
incident to himself, for the time being at least.

The next morning, as he gave his reconnaissance report to Lieutenant-Colonel Armstrong,
Pete described his visit as uneventful. That was a
lie, a big one at that, and one that Pete had waited
twenty-four hours to tell, but Armstrong had
ordered Pete to stay clear of anything to do with
Khan. The threat level was as high as it usually
was, but Pete let on that he'd observed no signifi-

cant change to the pattern of life in southern Panjwayi. Operation Open Highway, he reported, was good to proceed.

Pete did not tell his boss about what had kept him awake through the entire night. The sniper's voice, over the radio, *They are dragging young children out of the house.* His own voice saying, *Do not intervene.* Those words played in his head, over and over, like a mocking refrain. He'd made the correct call, he knew. He absolutely knew it. And yet he still felt shaky when it came to him.

Armstrong just nodded, clearly uninterested in Pete's sanitized report. Armstrong was booked on a transport plane out of KAF that very evening. His eyes—his entire posture—were already drinking a beer at a beachside bar. Pete couldn't really blame him. Everybody, from the bottom to the top, needed to take leave. Leaning back in his chair, lacing his hands over his midsection, Armstrong said, "Nice work, Pete. Looks good. You're on the right track."

"You're all packed to go, sir?"

"Yes I am."

"Well," said Pete, "have a cold one for me. Or two. Anyway, there are some backbriefs happening with General Rilmen after lunch, so I better get ready."

Pete shook Armstrong's hand. At Armstrong's door, Pete came to attention and then turned to leave. At the very moment he started to step away, Armstrong said, "Just a second, Pete."

Pete turned back around. "Sir?"

"I forgot to mention, intelligence has been tracking some interesting reports lately. Haji Malik—does that mean anything to you?"

Pete kept his face unreadable. He didn't think he was being tested—Armstrong didn't have the guile for that—but he had to be careful. "The Lion of the Desert, right? The Ghost?"

"These guys always have rock star names, don't they," said Armstrong. "Anyway, yes. Multiple sources have been saying that he's back in Kandahar from God knows where. I would've thought he'd died a long time ago. He would have to be in his sixties now. *If* it's even him. At any rate, keep your eyes open while I'm away."

"Will do, sir."

"And Pete, one last thing."

"Sir," said Pete.

"I meant what I said the other day. Stay out of

trouble. A little bit of office work wouldn't hurt."

Pete smiled blandly. "You got it, sir."

---

At thirteen hundred hours, no fewer than thirty people were crammed into the task force HQ conference room, giving Brigadier-General Rilmen a backbrief on the preparations for Operation Open Highway. The staff had been hard at work, and the presentation had almost a hundred PowerPoint slides. Even with the air conditioning, the conference room was very hot. Pete, as always, was packed in with the backbenchers in the corner of the room.

Despite the length of the backbrief and the sheer number of slides, the proposed operation was pretty simple. The battle group, with Charlie Company in the lead from Sperwan Ghar, would secure Hyena Road. The public affairs people would ensure that all the embedded journalists were there so the story could make the papers and TV news back home. The liaison staff would work with local elders to get their participation; everybody's favourite chairman of the provincial council, Bashir Daoud Khan himself, had of course promised his presence. Finally, General Rilmen and his sergeant major would arrive by road in the general's personal LAV patrol, call sign Niner Niner Tac.

"We've assessed that it would be safer for you to travel by helo, sir," said one of the officers at the table. "The IED threat on Hyena is severe. Even if the battle group secures the road, there are lots of blind—"

Rilmen slapped the tabletop with one of his gigantic hands. The sound was like a gunshot. Anybody who'd been dozing in the heat was instantly woken up. "No!" snapped Rilmen. "I told you in the beginning, I'm fucking well *driving* down there. That's the whole fucking point. Anybody who has an issue with that can talk to me after. Is that clear?"

The officer who'd suggested the helo went red in the face. "Yes sir," he muttered, looking down at his notebook.

The backbrief went on. There would be a quick ribbon-cutting ceremony, some words of dedication, some handshakes, some photographs, some interviews, some tea—and that would be that. Hyena Road would be formally dedicated to the great people of Panjwayi, of Kandahar, of Afghanistan.

General Rilmen, Pete thought, would have his Alexandria.

After another fifteen minutes of questions, the backbrief concluded just short of fourteen hundred. There was the usual hubbub as the meeting broke up and everybody got to their feet and milled around and chatted with each other.

Pete was about to step out of the conference room when Rilmen's voice cut over the crowd. "Where's my effects guy? Captain Martin, where are you?"

The room went quiet. All eyes snapped onto Pete. "Mitchell, sir."

"Right," said Rilmen. "Mitchell. Come on, we need to have a chat."

---

A few minutes later, Pete found himself in General Rilmen's office, three doors down from the conference room. The office was almost the same size and configuration as the conference room—same polished plywood walls, same windows overlooking the memorial—but in place of the long table was a vast desk. In one corner of the room was a sitting area; two overstuffed chairs faced a sofa with a small coffee table between them.

The sitting area might have been offered to dignitaries or senior allies, but Pete was pretty much left standing on one side of the desk as Rilmen sat down in a swivel chair on the other side. Sergeant Major Shorty sat down on top of a low mini-fridge nearby.

For a minute, Rilmen did nothing but study some papers on his desktop. Pete stood there, wondering if word of his exploits had somehow bypassed Armstrong and gotten to Rilmen. But instead of exploding, Rilmen took on an uncharacteristically meditative expression. When he spoke, his voice was softer than usual: "Truth is, Captain Mitchell, Hyena is still a mess. A gravel truck hit an IED this morning. Killed the contractor flat-out. He was from Kabul. Father of how many, Shorty?"

"Five, sir," said the sergeant major.

"Five. Christ. Fighting these pricks is like trying to nail Jell-O to the wall. Have you ever tried to nail Jell-O to the wall, Mitchell?"

Pete looked for any trace of mirth on the general's face. There was none. "I can't say as I have, sir."

"I can't keep losing people on that road," said Rilmen. "Civilians especially. Hyena has to go through. It's the only way for us to get the tanks down there, the only way to blow up the Taliban command and control and ratlines from Pakistan, the only way to smash their weapons caches, the only way to blow the fuckers out of their beds. I cannot do that bouncing around in helicopters. This is the *kinetic imperative*, Mitchell."

"Yes, sir."

"But the kinetic does not work without the non-kinetic. This is where you effects guys come in. I've heard that you in particular are one well-connected son-of-a-bitch. Is that true?"

"You could say that, sir. I've got a good network."

"What can you tell me?" said Rilmen.

Pete took a shallow breath. His mouth was dry. He glanced out the window. A cargo plane was lifting off from the KAF airstrip at that very moment. There was no way Armstrong was on it—nothing in real life fit together *that* nicely—but the lumbering plane was almost an omen all the same.

"Well, sir," said Pete. "If I can be candid here, my local guys are saying that Bashir Daoud Khan is a prominent figure in all this shit."

A tense beat. Rilmen and the sergeant major shared a quick look.

Sorry, Armstrong, thought Pete.

"Bashir Daoud Khan," said Rilmen, "is a fucking horrible little man. Every time I shake his hand I'd rather choke him."

"He profits from an unstable security situation," said Pete. "He extorts all the contractors, so the more times they have to go down Hyena to fill blast-craters, the more money he makes. It's ISAF paying the contractors, sir, as I'm sure you know. And lots of my guys are saying Khan blessed the attacks in Kandahar City last week . . ."

"And I've had some reports that he might not even show up for the dedication ceremony," said Rilmen, face darkening. "Just to fucking spite me. Shorty and I might have to lay a bet on it. Anyhow, you've just confirmed what I already know, Mitchell. And as I'm sure *you* know, barring some natural fucking disaster, we're stuck with Mr. Khan."

"I know it, sir."

"So what else can you tell me that I might be able to use?"

*I don't have much else, sir, unfortunately*, was what Pete intended to say. *I don't have much else, sir. I don't intervene, sir.*

Instead, after another shallow inhalation, he heard himself saying, "Are you familiar with the Lion of the Desert, sir?"

Another look between the general and the sergeant major. When Rilmen turned back to Pete, his expression was cool, penetrating, predatory. "I've heard of him, yes. Go on."

"Sir," said Pete, "could I bother you for a bottle of water, if you have any in here? I'm parched."

Both Rilmen's and Shorty's eyebrows lifted at the exact same time. Rilmen gestured. Shorty reached down between his legs and opened the mini-fridge and came out with a bottle of water. "Captain," he said, tossing it Pete's way.

Pete caught the bottle and opened it and took a drink. He was parched, that was true, but the slight digression had bought him a few precious seconds to get his thoughts in order—to contemplate exactly what in the hell he was about to do.

"The Lion of the Desert, the Ghost," said Pete, "is back. I believe he's in Kandahar City as we speak."

"Intelligence says his return is unconfirmed," said Rilmen. "Hell, half of the analysts think it's just urban legend. You're saying you know different?"

"My local guys are all pretty adamant that he's back. In fact one of them has family connections to him."

Shorty, openly doubtful, cut in: "Wouldn't he be old as dirt, Captain?"

"He's in his sixties," said Pete. The implication of that—*Not much more than ten years older than you two, and a muj his whole life*—didn't need to be articulated. Sergeant Major Shorty betrayed a quick scowl.

"Is he a threat?" Rilmen asked.

"No sir," said Pete. "The opposite. He pretty famously rebuffed the Taliban in the nineties, and even Mullah Omar had too much respect for him to fuck with him. I think he could be a pretty powerful ally."

"And why is that?"

Pete took a long drink of water and cleared his throat. "Well, sir, there's . . . history . . . between the Ghost and Bashir Khan. I think he might be able to bring Khan to heel, especially down around Hyena. If we could get the two of them together . . ." Rilmen was maintaining that penetrating look. Behind him, Shorty was studiously examining his fingernails. "This is the real non-kinetic stuff, sir," said Pete. "This is high-level hearts and minds."

At that Rilmen grinned. It was a savage, wolf-like grin, and it didn't exactly touch his eyes. "Okay, Captain Mitchell. I'm not convinced this guy isn't a myth, and I think half the analysts would laugh you out of the room, but I like what you're saying. You seem more willing to get your hands dirty than your boss does, at any fucking rate. So I don't care how you do it, get your Ghost and Khan talking, whatever, just make it so the civilians aren't getting hit every time they drive a truck down my fucking road."

---

Out in the Boneyard, the cleaner was vigorously squeegeeing the dull metal sides of the sea can office.

"Haji," said Pete. "What in the hell are you doing?"

The cleaner didn't stop his furious scrubbing. "You cannot see the paint job."

"It's a goddamn metal box—there's no paint job to see."

"Not the way it is, no."

Pete managed a thin laugh. He rocked back on his heels, rubbing his eyes. He felt like he *should* want a cigarette, and yet the idea still disgusted him. He hadn't had one since Sperwan Ghar. A couple of planes roared past overhead. Fighters, both of them, neither of them transports. It was almost suppertime; maybe Armstrong was gone and maybe not.

Either way, thought Pete, fuck him. He said, "I need your uncle to get in touch with the Ghost. I have an idea. It's, well, call it *badal* without bloodshed. We need to meet with him if it's at all possible. Not in the city this time. We'll use that safe house down in Panjwayi."

The cleaner turned around slowly. He held the

squeegee by his waist. The sponge was dripping filthy water onto the hard-packed ground. "You have approval for this, Pete?"

"Ah, more or less. Anyway it's always better to ask for forgiveness than permission, you know that."

# 12

RYAN WAS IN THE SPERWAN GHAR GYM in the evening, letting Tank put him through a gruelling workout. He hadn't been out on a patrol in what felt like ages; only a muscle-tearing workout seemed to do anything for this anger in his heart and restlessness in his soul.

"Two more reps, Warrant," said Tank. "That's it."

Ryan hissed through his teeth, curling a barbell up to his shoulders and back down again. Once. He was not able to finish the last repetition. He dropped the barbell back into its rack. Tank offered him a bottle of water and clapped him on the arm. "Now we do triceps," the big sniper said.

"I hate to interrupt this bromance, fellas."

Ryan looked over. Travis was standing there, watching him with faint amusement on his face. "What's up?" said Ryan.

"Captain Bowman's looking for you."

"Yeah, well, I don't have anything to say to her."

"She said you'd say that," said Travis. "And she said if that's the case, I'm supposed to drag your ass over to her."

Ryan shook his head. Out of the corner of his eye he could see Tank trying to hide a grin. "Do you need overwatch, boss?"

"Fuck off, bud," said Ryan.

- - -

Jenn was waiting where Travis had said she'd be, in one of the camp chairs near the ball hockey rink. The daylight was fading by the minute and the big floodlights were coming on. Ryan approached, not hurrying, not delaying. Maybe she wanted to talk about that upcoming operation, Open Road or Open Highway or whatever the hell they were calling it. Maybe she wanted to talk about other things. Either way, his guard was up.

He stopped short of where she was sitting. "Trav said you were looking for me," he said. He noticed then the crease on her forehead, the way she was staring off at nothing. Something was bothering her. He felt his guard soften a little. "Look," he said. "I'm sorry I lost my shit. But you know me, Jenn, and you know that most of the time I'm proud of what we do here, proud of how we go about doing it. But those were just little kids. If we can't help them, what's the point of all of this?"

She looked at him, seemed to take in his sweat-darkened PT clothes. "Sorry to interrupt your workout. Anyway, why don't you sit." Not a question. He lowered himself into the camp chair beside her. She sighed and said, "I don't have an answer about those little girls. For what it's worth I agree with you. In fact, if I think about it for even one second it eats me up . . . But that's not what I wanted to see you about."

"Oh," said Ryan. "So what is it?"

"You asked me about why I went to the med station."

"Yeah. Are you okay?"

Jenn was holding something out to him. Ryan looked down. It was her iPad, contained in a tough weatherproof casing. He took hold of it. The iPad was displaying an image, some kind of black mass in the midst of a wavy sea of grey. It was almost like a UAV freeze-frame—but he knew a UAV freeze-frame wasn't what he was seeing. He pulled his eyes away from the iPad and looked up at some moths swarming in the floodlights. He tried to order his thoughts and couldn't. All he could manage was to say, "What is this?"

"It's our baby," said Jenn. The crease across her forehead had deepened. Her eyes were hard and shining, not looking at him.

Ryan traced his fingers across the screen. He was delicate about it, as if he could actually feel the life in the image before him. He took a long, shaky breath. "Jenn," he said. "This is the most beautiful thing I have ever seen."

Now she did look at him, and the crease in her forehead disappeared and her features almost broke. Almost—but not quite. She needed to hold it together here, as did he. She dropped her hand beside her chair. He dropped his. Their fingers intertwined and squeezed tight.

"Changes things, doesn't it?" she whispered.

"It changes everything."

"And . . . ah . . . in terms of the brass I think we'll be fine because it happened when we were on leave. But we have to figure out what we're going to do." Jenn was talking quickly, probably as quickly as the thoughts were coming into her head.

"What do you mean, what we're going to do? We're going to have a baby."

"Is that what you want?"

Ryan smiled. He felt good. He almost felt like laughing out loud, like shouting up at the sky. That would be a good way to draw attention. "Yeah, that's what I want. More than anything."

"Okay. Okay. Good. I'm glad. I've been making myself crazy."

"What did you think I'd think?"

"I didn't *know*. Things between us were all fucked up, and—"

He squeezed her hand. "Things between us were fucked up. That's true. But like you say, this changes everything. Everything. We'll do what we have to do here, Jenn, and then we'll go home and have our baby. I love you."

She reached up and touched the corner of her eye. "I love you too, Ryan."

He wished there could be more; somewhere to take her and hold her. Somewhere they could just be alone. But there wasn't, not here in Sper.

These fleeting moments, these hidden touches, were all they had. And for now, they would have to be enough.

# 13

OPERATION OPEN HIGHWAY was a little less than a day away, but Pete Mitchell was thinking about *badal*. *Badal* without bloodshed.

The safe house stood alongside a lonely dirt track two kilometres south of Hyena Road, four kilometres east of Haji Baba, and three kilometres away from anything else. It was, in other words, the middle of nowhere. The mud-brick walls of the house looked poorly tended, and half of the roof had fallen in. To one side of the building was a copse of yew trees; to the other side was an astonishingly beautiful growth of wild sunflowers, standing shoulder-high. The sky overhead was as hard as ever. Tall pillars of red dust stood in the air above the Registan in the south.

Three Ford Rangers bounced along the dirt track and came to a stop in front of the neglected structure. As the plumes of dust settled, no fewer than a dozen ANA troops piled out of the vehicles. The troops moved into a defensive perimeter, training their AKs down the dirt track and over the open scrublands to the east and west. After another minute, Pete got out of the second vehicle. He was wearing his body armour and tac vest and helmet, and he had his C7 with him. On his back was the small patrol pack, the same one he'd toted through Kandahar City on the day of the attacks. By his side was Walid.

Pete took a moment to look around, gather his bearings. Across the scrubland to the west was a small saddleback ridge; at the base of the ridge, Pete could just make out a shepherd with a herd of goats, wavering in the heat, a scene out of ancient times. There was no one else in sight. "I guess he could stand us up," Pete said, mostly to himself.

Almost immediately, Walid said, "He is here."

Pete turned around. The Ghost was standing in the crooked doorway of the safe house. His strange eyes—his whole face—were unreadable.

- - -

There was a faint smell of old cooking oil and woodsmoke inside the safe house. The interior was barren of any furniture. No rugs, no lamps, nothing. Light fell in thick shafts, dust motes sparkling, through the windows and broken roof. Pete had brought his thermos of tea and three cups. He took off his helmet and lowered himself to the floor. He shrugged off his patrol pack and laid it at his side. Walid sat down beside him. Across from them sat the Ghost, cross-legged, giving away no sign of the old injury to his leg.

Pete cleared his throat. In his best Pashto, he said, "Thank you for meeting with me."

"The honour is mine," said the Ghost.

Pete gave a slight nod to show his acceptance of the compliment. He had had doubts that the Ghost would agree to meet in the first place, given what had happened in Haji Baba. So far none of Pete's contacts had been able to turn up any sign of the girls. They're long gone already, Pete thought. On the heels of that came a fleeting image of *where*, *what* the little girls were gone into. He recoiled at the image.

Meanwhile, the Ghost was looking around the empty interior of the safe house. He spoke a few words in Pashto. His tone was thoughtful, almost nostalgic.

"He says he is surprised to be sitting here," said Walid. "He says he was inside this house many times. He asks if you know who used to own this house."

"I do," said Pete. "Mullah Omar used to own this house. He gave lessons to his students right here."

Walid started to translate into Pashto but the Ghost held up a hand to stop him. Apparently Mullah Omar's name was enough. The Ghost said something.

"Omar saved his ears but he lost his eye," said Walid.

"That's an interesting thing to say," said Pete. "What does that mean?"

"Same same," said Walid.

"Same what, Haji?"

Before Walid could ask, the Ghost held up the arresting hand again. He sipped the tea from the Styrofoam cup Pete had offered him. He spoke.

"He wants you to talk now," said Walid. "What is the word? Speak your mind?"

Pete sipped his own tea. He had a sense that

the Ghost was testing him. He had a further sense that the Ghost's patience would quickly evaporate if Pete failed the test, whatever it was. "We own this house now," said Pete. Walid translated. Pete continued, "We own much of the land around it, too. If you should ever want to use this house, for whatever reason, it is yours."

The implication of Pete's offer was simple— this house, as derelict as it was, was not in Haji Baba and not in Kandahar City. Bashir Daoud Khan had no claim to it. This house could be used for discreet interactions. The Ghost gave an almost imperceptible nod of his head.

"There was an event in Panjwayi not long ago," said Pete. "In a village called Haji Baba. Two little girls were taken from the arms of their father."

He waited while Walid translated first his words and then the Ghost's. "He says these events are sadly common. He asks why you want to tell him about it."

"The little girls were taken by Bashir Daoud Khan," said Pete. The Ghost's face still gave nothing away. Pete let a moment pass by, carefully pacing his words before he spoke them. Then he said, "I know you have known Bashir Daoud

Khan for many years, Haji Malik. I know you commanded him in the Arghandab battles near Sangsar against the Soviets. I know he brought dishonour to your cause. And I know he was punished by your own hand, exiled to Pakistan."

There was the briefest, faintest movement around the corners of the Ghost's mouth. A *smile*, humourless but a smile all the same, gone as soon as it appeared. Pete almost believed he'd imagined it. The Ghost said something. Walid translated: "He said only Allah can judge for the punishment he gave to Khan."

"Yes," said Pete. "Because in some ways, that punishment made Khan into what he is today . . . Haji Malik, you must know that it is difficult for ISAF to deal with Bashir Daoud Khan."

After Walid translated, the Ghost just shrugged. He removed a fig from the pocket of his vest and set about peeling it. He didn't say anything, and he didn't need to. ISAF's dealings with Khan were of no concern to him.

"My general is a compassionate man," said Pete. "He is a student of Pashtunwali. He would like to help you, to help all Afghans. And to help the village of Haji Baba. He would be honoured if you would accept this gift." Pete opened his patrol pack and set it before him. It was, once again, densely packed with American money. "This is five thousand dollars," said Pete.

At once, the Ghost fixed Pete with a sharp, direct stare, and Pete wondered if he'd failed the test. He'd revealed what he knew about the Ghost's past with Khan, but he'd said nothing about the Ghost's family. The cash—the exact amount of Abdul's debt—was what spoke for him. Still, it was maybe too far. Pete met the Ghost's stare and held it.

Finally, in halting English, the Ghost said, "As before, I say now, only a fool accepts a gift without knowing what it is for."

"Consider it an exchange, then," said Pete.

"For what?"

"My general would be honoured if you would attend a ceremony for the opening of Hyena Road tomorrow morning."

The Ghost leaned back. When he replied, it was in Pashto again. Walid translated: "He says, why me? He says he is just a simple grape farmer."

"You're a respected elder of the region," said Pete. "Your presence would bring great honour to my general and to the road he has built."

The Ghost asked a question. Walid translated: "He asks who else will be at the ceremony."

The Ghost knew the answer already, of course. Pete was sure of that. But it was nevertheless part of the test.

"Bashir Daoud Khan," said Pete. No translation was necessary. Pete went on: "You will stand with my general, as will Khan. You will *both* be seen as sons of Kandahar. You may even meet with Khan privately, before the ceremony, as you see fit. Right here, for example."

Walid translated, and this time there was no mistaking it. The Ghost was smiling thinly. He replied in his halting English, "Thank your general for this kind offer. It will be my honour to attend."

---

Pete watched as the Ghost strode away across the scrubland. The old muj's limp was evident. He was heading in the direction of Haji Baba, and this time he had the patrol pack full of money with him. The farther away he got, the more he became one with the harsh landscape around him. Like a ghost, Pete thought. The notion amused him.

Pete put his helmet on and palmed sweat from the back of his neck.

He glanced at his watch. It was just past ten hundred. Less than twenty-four hours until Operation Open Highway would commence. He spoke a few words to the ANA platoon commander; the platoon commander called his cordon back in. The troops started to load back into their trucks. Pete and Walid made their way back to the second Ranger and opened the doors. As Pete started to climb into the truck, it occurred to him that a large part of him had not thought the Ghost would agree to this proposal. It was worth a try, he'd thought, but agreement might be a bridge too far. And yet the Ghost had agreed. For a second, Pete wondered what he'd set in motion—and whether it could possibly go as he'd planned.

The ANA driver was looking at Pete expectantly. Pete looked back to the surrounding countryside, the saddleback ridge in the west. It wasn't a kilometre away; was in fact less than that, maybe six or seven hundred metres. A sightline from the top of the saddleback would look straight at the safe house's front door.

Pete got into the truck. "Let's go," said Pete to the driver. Then, to Walid he said, "These guys will take you to KAF, but I need to go somewhere else."

# 14

Twelve hours left until Operation Open Highway was to commence.

"All right, guys," said Ryan. "Listen up."

He was standing at the head of the snipers' weather haven. All his detachments were seated before him. Jenn was present, as well, sitting on a corner of the map table. And standing beside Ryan was Pete Mitchell. The snipers were all unusually quiet; the presence of that troublesome effects captain was weighing hard on what was otherwise their little sanctuary. They were all looking to Ryan for an explanation.

It was almost suppertime. Outside, the light had the first golden tinges of evening. Sperwan Ghar was humming with activity as the rest of Charlie Company conducted rehearsals and preparations for the operation. Soldiers were crawling all over their LAVs, checking the communications equipment, the tires, the turrets, and the weapons systems; the cranky company quartermaster was barking at anyone who brought him a late requisition form; the platoon commanders were checking and rechecking their maps; everybody else was cleaning their rifles.

Ryan continued: "There's a slight change of plans to what we're doing for tomorrow's op. It really only affects my own det . . ."

At that moment, Ryan noticed that Travis wasn't looking at him. Trav was looking at Pete Mitchell. He appeared calm, but there was high colour in Trav's cheeks. An explanation was *definitely* needed.

It had been just after lunch when Pete had appeared. Unannounced as usual, and most likely a harbinger of some kind of disaster. Pete had been wearing his vest, had his helmet in one hand, his rifle slung over his back, and had sweated through his combats, as if he'd been out somewhere. On seeing him, Ryan had felt a series of things in quick succession: surprise, dismay, resignation, and a more-than-slight desire to punch Pete out. Up until that moment he'd felt only the incredulity he'd carried since his talk with Jenn—he was going to be a father.

*Ryan*, Pete had said.

*Captain Mitchell*, Ryan had flatly replied.

*I know I'm probably the last person you want to see, but if you can hear me out for one minute, I'm working on a way to make things right, and I need your help.*

"Master Corporal Davidson?" said Ryan. "Are you with me?"

Travis's gaze switched back to Ryan. He nodded. "Yeah, Warrant. Sorry."

"Okay," said Ryan. "Originally we were going to drop an observation post on the north side of Hyena, but if you look here"—he pointed to a spot on the map—"there's a small high feature. We will be able to observe the dedication ceremony from the top of this high feature, although at double the distance than I'd planned. But this high feature overlooks an abandoned building, here." He pointed nearby on the map.

"What's the range?" said Tank.

"A bit long," said Ryan. "Fifteen hundred metres to the dedication ceremony, but only seven hundred to the abandoned building."

"What's so special about the building?" said Travis.

"It's a safe house," said Ryan. "It's our asset."

Again Ryan saw Travis's eyes flick over to Pete, and again that colour heightened in Trav's face. Travis was well aware of the turmoil that usually came with Captain Mitchell. Not to mention that Pete had been the one to prevent Travis from engaging when Khan was taking the girls away. Ryan didn't know if that was something he or Travis or anyone could ever get over.

*I'm working on a way to make things right, and I need your help*, Pete had said. That was the only reason Ryan had heard him out—and the only reason Ryan was standing in front of his snipers now, briefing them on the change in plans. A way to make things right.

"What are we doing with the safe house, Warrant?" said Hickey.

"Observation," said Ryan. "Captain Mitchell here—ah, correction to that—*we* believe that two local national VIPs are going to show up at this safe house prior to the dedication ceremony. The VIPs are going to settle a monetary debt. How smoothly this meet-up goes will have a direct impact on the success of Op Open Highway."

"As well as security in the entire province," said Jenn. She had already been briefed, by Ryan and Pete both, and she'd thrown in her support. "Especially down around here."

Ryan nodded. "That's right. If you haven't guessed it already, one of the VIPs is Haji Malik, a.k.a. the Ghost, a.k.a. the guy who gave us shelter in Haji Baba. The other VIP is Bashir Daoud Khan, chairman of the provincial—"

"And fucking kidnapper," said Travis.

"Yeah," said Ryan. "Him."

A low rumble coursed through the assembled snipers.

"Wouldn't it just be better for everyone if we put this guy down?" said Travis.

Travis was obviously displeased and starting to get out of hand, which was not at all like him. Ryan was about to respond, was even ready to give Trav a mild upbraiding, when Pete cut in: "In some ways, yes, Master Corporal. I think so myself, as does just about anyone else you would ask. But it doesn't work like that."

Travis glared at Pete but kept his voice even. "Then how does it work with this guy, sir?"

Pete looked at Ryan. Ryan nodded. Pete cleared his throat. "Bashir Daoud Khan is a gangster, but he's *our* gangster. Here's what you should know about him . . ."

Everyone listened as Pete described Bashir Daoud Khan's biography to them. Pete worked backwards, starting with Khan's business interests, both legal and otherwise, Khan's political connections going as far as the presidency in Kabul, and the lucrative relationships Khan had built with the CIA and Pakistani intelligence. From there Pete traced Khan back to the jihad against the Soviets, the incident with the Soviet helicopter pilot, and the legendary mujahedeen commander who'd exiled him for it.

"So you see," said Pete, "Khan and our Ghost have a long history together. The Ghost came back to Kandahar to raise the money to settle his son's account, which you guys observed—and yes, before you say it, it turned into a total disaster. That's on me. I underestimated Khan and that's on me." He trailed off, letting the admission sink in. Travis had not looked away from Pete for one second, but at least the angry glare had faded from Trav's eyes.

"Sir," said Tank, "how do you think the meeting between these guys is going to fix anything now?"

Pete nodded thoughtfully, scratching his chin. "Well, I'd originally thought it was as simple as trading Khan for the Ghost. It's not. Khan is too well-connected. He's not going anywhere. I guess I've made my peace with that, as much as I can. But with the Ghost back here, and with him as our newly visible ally to boot, Khan is no longer the top dog he's been for a long time. He *can't* be, not with his old commander here, the same guy who sent him away in disgrace. So Khan gets his money, his goddamn fucking five grand—and the Ghost gets the satisfaction of publicly seeing the prideful Khan taken down a notch, just like he did all those years ago when he exiled him. *Badal*—revenge—is served. And without bloodshed."

Another low rumble went through the snipers, this one sounding a little more speculative than the last. Not one of them, Ryan knew, had much use for these shadow war machinations, but they were at least somewhat intrigued by the history of Khan and the Ghost.

"So we just observe the safe house in case

they meet up there?" said Hickey. "What about extraction after it all goes so super-smooth?"

It was Jenn who answered. "Most of the company will be deployed along various points of Hyena Road, securing it for the dedication ceremony. Once you get the order to collapse, you guys will just come down off the back side of your high feature and meet up with the nearest platoon. It probably won't be more than two klicks away."

"And I'm going back out with Six-Six myself," said Ryan. He glanced at Pete. Ryan's deployment with his det was his own part of the deal, discussed with Pete and Jenn beforehand. He wanted to be with his guys this time, no matter what happened; he wouldn't be stuck in the CP. "So Wilf—where are you, bud?—you're sitting this one out."

"Roger, Warrant," said Wilf.

"We're deploying at midnight," said Ryan. "So if there are any questions, now's the time."

"I have one," said Travis. Ryan already knew what the question was going to be, but it was only fair to let Travis articulate it. He nodded, and Travis said, "What about those little girls?"

"This is all part of it," said Pete. "With the

monetary debt settled, and with the Ghost in an open position of power with ISAF, the pressure on Khan to return them safe and sound will be pretty intense. I . . . Look, I can't promise anything, but this way is our best bet."

Ryan looked for any trace of duplicity on Pete's face but there was none. Pete believed what he was telling them. And even if he didn't believe it, it didn't matter. This would almost certainly be the only chance Six-Six would have to make up for the kidnapping.

■ ■ ■

As the evening got late—twenty-one hundred became twenty-two hundred—Charlie Company concluded its preparations for Open Highway, and a strange, collective calm fell over Sperwan Ghar. It was always like this in the final hours before an operation commenced, even one as apparently straightforward as Open Highway. The calm was equal parts forced rest, inward reflection in every soldier's mind, and the simple lack of having anything else to do but wait for H-Hour.

Pete Mitchell had crashed in the transient

tent. Hickey was playing a game on his laptop. Tank was in the gym. Travis had just finished Skyping his wife and had gone to be by himself in the chapel, perhaps to ask God a thing or two about kidnapped children.

At twenty-two-ten, Jenn left the CP. Her body was leaden with exhaustion, but her mind was still buzzing with all the details of the company's deployment, now only hours away. She would be back in the CP for zero-four-thirty. But instead of going back to her tent and trying to sleep, she angled toward a concrete blast shelter on the far side of the common area. The interior of the blast shelter was utterly black, but Ryan was in there waiting. She could smell him. She fell into his arms and for a long time she just let him hold her.

"Weird day," he said after a while.

"Yeah," said Jenn.

"Everything's gone weird since I met the Ghost in Haji Baba. It's almost enough to make me superstitious."

"Everybody's superstitious on tour," said Jenn. "In some way or another. Lieutenant Brown won't put up any pictures of her family."

Ryan laughed quietly.

They both let another minute or two of comfortable silence pass, simply enjoying the closeness of each other's bodies and the relative cool of the evening air. Ryan's arms tightened around her. "We're going to have a baby," he whispered. "Jesus. I keep thinking about that. This big, bad world, and we're going to have a baby."

"I hope you're okay with that."

"Are you kidding? It's the best thing I've ever heard." He put his fingers on her chin and tilted her face up and kissed her. When they broke apart, he said, "Listen, this is crazy, but I'd like it very much if you'd marry me, Captain Bowman."

"That is crazy. Certifiable."

"Is that a yes?"

"Of course it's a yes, Warrant Officer Murphy. You knew that even before you asked."

They kissed again, long and deeply. She was the one who broke it off.

"Is something bothering you?" said Ryan.

"No . . . Yes. I don't know."

"Tell me."

"I just didn't expect to see Pete Mitchell down here again," said Jenn. "And I really didn't expect you to agree with him."

"I didn't either. But the thing is, I think his plan makes sense. For once. I believe it."

"I do too," said Jenn.

"See what I mean? Mitchell making sense, us believing him—it's a weird day all around." There was a brief spark of eerie blue light as Ryan glanced at his watch. He sighed. "Anyways, it's just about time to kit up."

Jenn moved in close to him again. She found the fly of his combat pants and unzipped it. "Let me help you with that kit."

She heard Ryan suck in his breath. She felt his hands move down her own body. They didn't have a lot of time, but they didn't *need* a lot of time, either. And far above the concrete blast shelter where they came together, the stars shone in their countless multitudes, as distant and indifferent as they were beautiful.

---

Far fewer stars shone over Kandahar City, if only because the city's own electric lights blotted the sky out. The city's glow at night was ugly and harsh, browned out in many quarters, over-bright in others. Hamid Wali Khan was shooting pool in the Madad Café near the city's central roundabout. The interior of the café was billowing with cigarette smoke and the smells of Turkish coffee, short-order chicken, and what passed for fast food. It was full of customers, all of them men, either crowded around the single television to watch cricket or hunched over the Internet terminals or playing billiards on the beat-up tables.

Hamid had just won his third game in a row—but he always won when he was playing against Nabil. "You're fucking terrible at this," Hamid chided.

Nabil, a gigantic man with sloping shoulders and an urn-shaped head, just chalked his cue glumly and didn't reply. They had a small amount of money riding on the game. It was *haram* to gamble, but it was also a hell of a lot of fun, and Hamid insisted. Besides, it was his father's money anyway—what both he and Nabil had to ante up.

Just then, Faisal and Ibrahim, both just as huge as Nabil (and as terrible at pool), pushed their way through the crowd and leaned in alongside the table. Faisal had his Roshan mobile phone in his hand. "Hamid," he said, "we have to go make our collections now."

"Now?" said Hamid. "It's an hour early."

"Our guy is ready now," said Faisal. "In another hour he probably won't even remember his own name."

Faisal was only slightly smarter than Nabil and Ibrahim, which wasn't saying much, but Hamid had to admit he had a point. Junkies—like the ones they were going to collect from—were notoriously unreliable.

"Ugh, all right," grunted Hamid. "One of you go pay the fucking tab."

---

Outside the café, the main drag was buzzing with motorbikes and auto-rickshaws and taxis. Anybody out walking at this hour was young and probably dangerous. But that was okay; Hamid Wali Khan knew he was the most dangerous of all. Nobody fucked with him. He sauntered down the sidewalk, flanked by his three daunting friends. He didn't know what his father paid them, but he didn't think it was much. It didn't need to be, either; if it wasn't for even the modest generosity of Bashir Daoud Khan, these three stone-brained brutes would be working the fields somewhere or, worse yet, enlisted in the bloody ANA.

The four of them turned off the main drag onto a dark, narrow side street. At once Faisal and Ibrahim pulled small automatic pistols out from under their vests. Nabil slid a spring-loaded leather sap out of his sleeve. All three of the men kept their weapons dangling at their sides. Hamid grinned. He had no need to pack anything himself when he had these guys to either do the shooting or to take the fall if they got stopped. His father had taught him this lesson. It felt good to carry a gun or a sap or a knife, yes, but it felt much better to be the one at the top. All of the world's most powerful men practised this.

They turned a corner and came in sight of a dilapidated building. The building had once been a medical clinic; now it was just one more cinder-block carcass. The interior of the building wasn't completely black—there were little sparks of light here and there. Candles and cigarette lighters. As Hamid knew, anywhere from ten to a hundred junkies were holed up in the ruin. The guy they'd come to meet was himself a junkie, but he was at least a little more intact than all the others, enough that he could act as middleman, collector, and user all in one.

Hamid and his three companions came to a stop on a deserted corner across from the building. They waited for a few minutes. Then, impatiently, Hamid called out, "Hey, *bacha bazi*, where the fuck are you?"

He strode forward a few paces.

"Hamid," murmured Faisal, "don't go too far."

Hamid laughed. "The only thing around here are a bunch of dirty junkies."

"You should stay close to us, man," said Faisal.

"What are you afraid of?" Hamid said over his shoulder. "Some fucking *ghosts*?"

He turned back around and faced the building. Nobody had emerged yet. In fact, all the little points of light—candle flames and cigarette lighters—had disappeared. Now the interior of the building was completely black. This didn't seem right. He frowned.

His friends moved up on either side of him. He started to say something, and then Ibrahim's big hands took hold of his arms. Hamid shut up.

This didn't seem right at all, but he couldn't quite make sense of it. Headlights came to life at the other end of the street. A small van appeared. He tried to step back as the van advanced toward him, but Ibrahim held him tight. At that moment it dawned on Hamid that Ibrahim's hold on him was not protective. Not at all. The van pulled to a stop beside them, and someone inside slid the side door open. Hamid could make out the silhouettes of at least two men inside, but he could see nothing of their faces.

Finally Hamid started to squirm and shout, but almost at once a scrap of cloth was yanked hard over his mouth. He could feel fingers tying the cloth in a knot at the back of his head. His eyes rolled. It was Faisal—fucking *Faisal*—tying the knot!

They were already hauling him backwards, off his feet, to the van's open side door. Hamid kicked and tried to struggle, but it was no use, not against the three brutes. His protests became screams, only thinly muffled by the gag. But this was a bad part of a bad city, and only dangerous people were out this time of night, and nobody paid him the least bit of attention.

As they got him through the door, into the arms of the unknown men within the van, Nabil stepped forward. The man's lips curled back. "You know something, boss? I fucking hate playing pool, and gambling is *haram*." Nabil brought the leather sap down on Hamid's head, hard enough to knock the younger Khan into a cross-eyed stupor.

■ ■ ■

A minute later the van was gone. Hamid Wali Khan was trussed and gagged and unconscious inside it. Nabil, Faisal, and Ibrahim all left the side street outside the junkie den by different directions. Each of them was richer now by a three-way split of five thousand American dollars.

# 15

June 20th—D-Day for Operation Open Highway—dawned clear, with very little wind and no risk of sandstorms. The weather had been the final potential showstopper for the operation; if there were a low-hanging overcast or if a sandstorm occurred, all flights, including medevac, would have to be grounded, and thus the operation would have to be delayed or cancelled altogether. But there wasn't a single cloud in the sky that morning. At zero-five-thirty, Open Highway officially launched.

Charlie Company's LAV platoons rolled out of Sperwan Ghar at exactly their appointed times: 1 Platoon at five-thirty-five, 2 Platoon at five-forty-five, and 3 Platoon at five-fifty-five. Each platoon was to stagger itself in overwatch positions along a six-kilometre stretch of Hyena

Road, creating as secure a corridor as possible.

At the eastern end of the secure corridor was a tiny collection of houses and shops and other buildings, marking the very first section of Hyena Road to be constructed, some months before. It was here that the dedication ceremony would take place. A humble mud-brick schoolhouse had been chosen as the backdrop. By zero-six-thirty, a dozen local elders as well as five Kandahari journalists had already showed up and were milling outside the schoolhouse. Before the attendees had gotten within a hundred metres of the site, they'd all been searched by Afghan cops and Canadian Charlie Company soldiers. The body searches might have been poorly received had not every single person in the province already been through them countless times before. Body searches came with ISAF.

In any case, the heightened security seemed to be working. Nothing had happened on Hyena Road or in the surrounding environs for the last twenty-four hours. Not even one IED had been upturned. All was calm.

Brigadier-General Rilmen was on his way.

---

Back at Sperwan Ghar, Jenn had given Pete a small corner of the CP where he could listen in on the radio and stay on top of the situation at the safe house. She was concerned about the safe house as well, but she also had the rest of the company to manage, and communications higher with the battle group and task force besides. She'd also given Pete a ground rule: no transmitting on the net without her say-so. Last time hadn't gone so well.

Six-Six had been in place since zero-three-hundred, and for over four hours they'd had nothing to report. As far as they could tell, the safe house was vacant. Pete lurked in his little corner of the CP, scratching his chin. Maybe the safe house was a red herring; maybe the Ghost and Khan would show up at the dedication ceremony, just like they'd both said they would. He squeezed his eyes shut. There were enough variables here, enough what-ifs, to make anyone crazy.

At the present moment, the central focus of everyone else in the CP was the dedication ceremony. The platoon commanders on the ground had just reported that all their assets were in place.

More locals were trickling in. The crowd around the schoolhouse had swollen to forty or fifty. There were no danger indicators yet, no problems with the pattern of life. The battle group had delegated two UAVs to Charlie Company, and the signallers had the feeds up on the screens in the CP. What was shown was the site of the ceremony from a bird's-eye view, sometimes switching to a hazy close-up. People moved around like little blobs, making Pete think of the archived footage of the artillery strike outside Haji Baba—the incident that had caused this whole mess.

"Can I get a sitrep on Niner Niner Tac?" said Jenn.

Niner Niner Tac was Rilmen's personal convoy. The duty NCO listened into his headset for a moment, then said, "Ten mikes out, ma'am."

Jenn glanced at the map board, then turned back to the duty NCO. "And have any of the VIPs shown up at the schoolhouse yet?"

The duty NCO relayed the query down to the platoons on the ground. He waited a moment, listening, and then shook his head. "No ma'am. Some local elders, some journalists from the city, a bunch of civilians—that's all."

Jenn looked at Pete. "How do you think this is going to play out?"

"It might be too early to say one way or the other," said Pete.

"If the general gets to the schoolhouse and neither of the VIPs are there, he is not going to be happy."

"He knows how things work with these people," said Pete.

■ ■ ■

At seven-thirty, Niner Niner Tac—consisting of two LAVs—arrived at the schoolhouse. By then the assembly had grown to almost sixty people. The vast majority of them were locals who'd probably come for no other reason than to take a break from the monotony of farm work, but a few foreign correspondents had also arrived.

Neither the Ghost nor Khan were anywhere to be seen.

Rilmen and Shorty and their personal security detachment, along with half a dozen staff officers, came down from the back of the LAVs. The staff officers, in particular, looked unaccustomed to wearing their body armour and carrying their weapons. Two of them immediately set about stretching a bright yellow ribbon across the road. They tied it to a crooked telephone post on one side, and on the other side they jammed the end of the ribbon between the bricks in the corner of the schoolhouse wall. The crowd of locals watched.

Rilmen and Shorty, meanwhile, were making the rounds, grinning, shaking hands with the elders. "Salaam alaikum, salaam alaikum," Rilmen kept saying, and then to Shorty, through his teeth, "The goddamn VIPs aren't gonna show."

"Oh, I think they'll be here, sir," said Shorty. "It's important to them."

"Salaam alaikum," Rilmen said to an ancient-looking elder. "And twenty-five bucks, Shorty, says they're a no-show."

"You're on, sir."

Rilmen got down on one knee to shake hands with two young boys. He grinned at them, said, "Salaam alaikum." The boys smiled back at him. Rilmen stood. "I love your enthusiasm, Shorty. Also, I'm going to choke that effects captain if I'm left standing here with my dick in my hand. What's his name? Martin?"

"Mitchell, sir. Captain Mitchell."

"Right," said Rilmen. "Mitchell."

---

From Six-Six's hide on the saddleback ridge, the site of the dedication ceremony was just visible. At that range, fifteen hundred metres to the northwest, it was difficult to make out fine details, even through their optics. Sergeant Major Shorty and Brigadier-General Rilmen looked like a pair of mismatched ants in the midst of a crowd of local ants. Hickey and Tank were observing that direction, Hickey with the .308 and Tank with a spotter's scope.

"They *actually* have a fucking ribbon to cut," Hickey mused. "Unbelievable. I'd say they were going to break out the champagne too, but look where we are."

Observing to the east were Ryan and Travis. This time Travis had the spotter's scope, and Ryan was on the Tac-50. Through the scope, the safe house reared up from the surrounding scrubland. The patch of sunflowers glittered brightly in the morning sun, but the safe house itself was dark and apparently lifeless, as it had been all night.

Six-Six's insertion had been long but uneventful. The snipers had travelled only a short distance on Hyena Road from Sperwan Ghar before breaking south through the dusty plains and grape fields, and then doglegging northeast to the saddleback. It was eerily similar to the route by which they'd exfiltrated on the day they'd ended up in Haji Baba.

Ryan leaned back from his scope and wiped sweat out of his eyes. "Hey, Hickey, still no VIPs on your side?"

"That's a negative, boss," said Hickey.

Ryan thumbed his MBITR. "Three Niner Alpha, Golf Niner Whiskey, this is Six-Six. Sitrep. Nothing—"

Just then, Travis said, "Ryan, look."

"Wait out," Ryan said into his comms. He leaned back into his scope. There, standing in the doorway of the safe house, was the tall, lean figure of the Ghost. The range was too great to make out the old man's eyes, but the severe shape of his face was plainly visible. Ryan felt a chill run down his spine. *Where the hell did you come from?* he thought. *Were you in there all fucking night?*

"That's not all," Travis breathed. "Three fingers north, up the laneway. Look." Ryan looked. Three white Toyota Sequoia SUVs were charging down the rutted track toward the safe house. Dust plumed up behind them. "Ryan, those are the same trucks I saw take the kids away."

Ryan thumbed his comms. "Three Niner Alpha, Golf Niner Whiskey, this is Six-Six. Looks like we've got something here."

— — —

Back in the CP, Pete and Jenn listened in on their headsets as Ryan described what he was seeing. The up-armoured SUVs coming down the lane, the Ghost who'd appeared out of nowhere—Pete felt his pulse quicken and moisture break out on his hands. The meet-up was happening.

"Three Niner Alpha, acknowledged," Jenn replied after Ryan had finished sending his sitrep. There was a slight edge in her voice. She stood up, slipping her headset down around her neck. She turned to Pete. "You're on."

Pete nodded. To the duty NCO he said, "Don't pass anything down to the dedication site yet. For all we know, the VIPs might conduct their business at the safe house first before going over to General Rilmen's location. I doubt they'd be hand in hand, exactly, but let's just wait out on that."

"Yes sir," said the duty NCO.

Pete keyed his headset. "Six-Six, this is Golf Niner Whiskey. I need you to confirm who you're observing ASAP . . ."

---

For the first time in more than twenty years, the old man was looking into the eyes of his former inferior, Bashir Daoud Khan. The intervening years had fattened Khan's face and given him a paunch around his midsection, but the derision in his eyes now was unchanged from all those years ago.

Behind Khan, half a dozen men climbed down from the parked SUVs. Black turbans, heavy beards—Talibs all of them. They arranged themselves in a loose semicircle behind their master. This brought grim amusement to the old man; he wondered if Mullah Omar had ever taught his students that it was acceptable to work for a bugger and crook like Khan. The Talibs were not visibly armed. They knew, as everyone else did, that the foreign coalition had eyes all the time—perhaps on top of that saddleback ridge in the middle distance, for example—and the sight of a naked weapon could be enough to bring the artillery down. Still, the Talibs' weapons were close, likely no further away than under their vests or in their SUVs.

"Salaam alaikum," said the old man.

"Spare the shit, Malik," Khan spat. He was holding the lapels of his pinstripe blazer, pacing back and forth in the dust. His fat face was purple with anger. Not just anger, but *fear*. "You arranged this. What do you want?"

"Bashir, you have insulted the honour of my family," the old man said calmly. "As a former fighter under my command, this is a great sin."

Khan spat into the dirt. "First of all, you never had the stomach for it in those days, old man. Second, your goat-fucker son owes me five thousand dollars. Why you got dragged out of the ground and into this, I don't understand. You should've stayed in Pesh or wherever the hell you were, because I doubt you have the stomach for it now."

The old man smiled. He reached down to the ground beside him. The Talibs behind Khan closed in a few paces, still not drawing any weapons—but all the old man fetched up from the ground was Pete Mitchell's patrol pack.

"Yesterday the foreigners gave me five thousand dollars," said the old man. As soon as he said it, Khan stopped pacing, eyeing the patrol pack with a mixture of greed and doubt. The pack looked like it had some weight to it. The old man continued, "Five thousand dollars is nothing to them, but they believe they can help settle the debt between us, and in so doing they will bring about peace."

Khan bared his teeth in a not-quite grin. "So here you are to pay up, then, with their money. Is that it?"

The old man held the pack up in both hands. Khan took a step forward, and immediately the old man brought the pack back down to his midsection. He said, "Before I give you this, I want my granddaughters returned."

Khan blinked. A moment passed. Khan and the nearest Talib shared a quick glance, then Khan looked at the old man. "They're gone, old man. Long gone. You know this. And you know, too, that it's Abdul's fault. I gave him more time than *anyone* deserves."

The old man lowered his head fractionally. Quietly, he said, "I am sorry to hear this."

He was sorry to hear it, but he was not surprised. Networks like Khan's moved quickly. It was the only way they could avoid interference. As Khan had said, the old man knew this. The old man had spent the entire night in the remnants of Mullah Omar's house. He'd been awake the whole time, sitting in the dark, thinking his shadowy thoughts. He'd been interrupted only once, a little after midnight, when Ghulam and some others had arrived from the city in Ghulam's van . . .

Khan's face purpled again. He jabbed his finger in the air. Spittle flew from his lips. "You better not be fucking with me, old man. I haven't heard from my own son since last night, and that's the only reason I haven't killed you already! Where is he? *I want to see my son!*"

The Ghost fixed his eyes on Khan. He pulled open the top flap of the patrol pack and reached inside. "So you shall see him, Bashir."

Ryan and Travis had observed the whole inter-action from the moment the SUVs had arrived and Khan and his men had gotten out, keeping any weapons they might have concealed. They'd observed as Khan and the Ghost talked to each other, the Ghost staying framed in the safehouse doorway, Khan in the dusty lane out front. They'd observed as the Ghost had reached down beside him and brought up a patrol pack. Ryan thought the patrol pack looked familiar; he remembered Pete carrying it to the bakery in Kandahar City.

Ryan sent periodic sitreps up, describing each thing he saw. Every time he heard Golf Niner Whiskey acknowledge, he could hear a rising ten-sion in Pete's voice. *Is this what you had in mind, Pete?* Ryan thought. Whatever was unfolding, it probably had the chance to become another Mitchell-style clusterfuck, and yet Ryan was oddly calm. As calm as he'd been in as long as he could remember.

On the other side of the hide, Hickey and Tank were still observing the dedication ceremony. It was just after eight-hundred hours now; General

Rilmen had to know his VIPs were pretty badly delayed, if they were showing up at all. Ryan didn't envy any of the officers in the general's immediate proximity.

"The Ghost is reaching into the bag," said Travis.

Ryan thumbed his comms. "Golf Niner Whiskey, this is Six-Six. Call sign Ghost is reaching into the bag. I'm guessing this is the five grand."

Pete's voice crackled back. "Golf Niner Whiskey, roger, keep the info coming."

The tension in Pete's voice, even over the net, sounded like it was getting close to a peak. Ryan backed off his scope a couple of centimetres. He couldn't help but smile a little.

"*Jesus Christ,*" Travis hissed.

Ryan put his eye back to the scope. It took him half a second to realize what he was seeing, hanging by the hair from the Ghost's hands. The features on the face were beaten beyond any recognition, but the mouth was hanging open and some kind of gold grill was flashing in the sun. Hideous red-black gore hung from the ragged base of the neck.

Ryan squeezed his eye shut, revulsion sweeping through him. When he opened his eye again, the horror in the Ghost's hands was still there.

---

The CP was utterly silent for what seemed a long time. At last Pete keyed his headset. "Six-Six, this is Golf Niner Whiskey. Say again?"

A brief delay, then: "Golf Niner Whiskey, this is Six-Six. I say again, it's a head, a human fucking head . . . I think it's the son, call sign Hotel Whiskey Kilo."

Pete leaned on the map table in front of him. Then he stood up straight. Then he leaned again. He put a hand to his forehead. Jenn was watching him. Everyone in the CP was watching him.

"Pete," said Jenn.

Things were surging through Pete's head at a breakneck pace. *Badal* without bloodshed—how could he have been so short-sighted? And yet . . . this? What in the hell was the Ghost doing? How could his honour be restored if—

"*Pete*," said Jenn.

Honour, Pete thought, and right away he knew exactly what the Ghost was doing. "Khan will react," Pete said, his voice scarcely more than a whisper. "He'll have to. But Ryan must not engage."

Watching Pete, Jenn keyed her headset. "Six-Six, Three Niner Alpha. I need a sitrep. What's Khan doing? Do you have hostile intent?"

■ ■ ■

"Six-Six," sent Ryan. "Negative. No hostile intent at this time. Am observing."

Through their optics, Ryan and Travis watched the front of the safe house, where a surreal drama was playing out. It had been no more than thirty seconds since the Ghost had pulled Hamid Wali Khan's severed head out of the patrol pack and tossed it into the dirt at the elder Khan's feet. The surrounding Talibs were standing there, seemingly at a complete loss as to what to do. Khan himself was on his knees—much like Abdul had been, the day they'd taken his daughters—pulling at his hair. And the Ghost was standing stolidly in the safe house doorway. Even through the scope, his face was ablaze with a wrath Ryan had never seen on anyone in his life. It was terrifying.

Abruptly Khan leapt to his feet. He stumbled into the Talib closest to him. He appeared to struggle with the man for a second. Then Khan pulled away from the Talib—and in his hands was the automatic pistol he'd pulled from under the Talib's vest.

"There it is," whispered Travis.

Ryan thumbed his comms. "Three Niner Alpha, Golf Niner Whiskey, this is Six-Six. Call sign Bravo Delta Kilo has a weapon."

Pete's voice came back immediately: "What's the Ghost doing?"

Ryan looked. The Ghost had taken a few steps outside the safe house and was standing in front of Khan. Hamid's head was at the Ghost's feet. Still that indescribable wrath burned on the Ghost's face.

"Golf Niner Whiskey, this is Six-Six," said Ryan. "The Ghost is just standing there."

"Six-Six, Golf Niner Whiskey," Pete replied tensely. "There's a reason he's just standing there. Do not take any action."

"Khan is gonna drop him," Travis said in a quiet voice.

Through the optics, they could see Khan struggling with the slide on the pistol. It looked like he wasn't used to handling a weapon on his own. The Ghost remained standing outside the door. Ryan did not understand what was happening between the two men; with this he realized he did not understand Pete Mitchell's shadow war at all. He never had. What he *did* understand was hostile intent against an unarmed civilian—an unarmed civilian who'd saved his life.

Ryan thumbed his comms. "This is Six-Six. I have imminent threat. I am engaging. Will advise."

When Pete's voice came back, it was cracked and panicked: "Six-Six, this is Golf Niner Whiskey. I'm overriding—"

Almost right away Jenn's voice cut in. "Six-Six, this is Three Niner Alpha. I acknowledge your last. Carry on."

Ryan smiled. Jenn understood too. He settled behind his rifle. Through his scope he watched as Khan managed to rack the slide on the pistol . . .

"Deflection is point nine," said Travis. "You're on."

Ryan made the minute adjustment, lined up the reticle, levered off the safety. "Standing by."

"Golf Niner Whiskey," came Pete's voice, pleading now. "Ryan, please do not take that fucking shot."

Khan lifted the pistol to the Ghost's chest.

"Send it," said Travis.

Ryan squeezed the trigger. The Tac-50 thundered and bucked his shoulder. There was half a second of nothingness—the bullet's travel time—and then the upper half of Bashir Daoud Khan's head dissolved in a red spray. The man dropped to the ground, the unfired pistol still in his hand. Around Khan's body, the Talibs were all ducking, bounding, scrambling for their SUVs, looking in every direction for the source of the shot that had just killed their boss.

The Ghost stood his ground. His face and beard were spattered with blood. His face was turned directly at the saddleback ridge. Ryan couldn't help but feel that the Ghost was staring straight at him.

---

Two thousand metres away, the crowd around the schoolhouse had begun to disperse. One of the Kandahari journalists was packing up his gear. Rilmen stood beside the gaudy yellow ribbon, trying to keep a congenial smile overtop a deepening scowl. A goat blithely wandered past, close enough to bump its hindquarters against Rilmen's leg. It was all the general could do to not haul out his sidearm and put the goat down.

Shorty, who'd been on the radio in the back of one of the LAVs, ambled over. He said, "Zero has no idea where the VIPs are, sir. Nobody can reach them. Apparently Captain Mitchell's over at Sper but he's not picking up either."

Rilmen nodded.

"I recommend we hit the road, sir," said Shorty.

Rilmen stood rooted to the spot for a full ten seconds. The scowl had totally overtaken his face. Any Canadians in the immediate vicinity knew to give him a wide berth. Even Shorty was staying a short distance away. All at once Rilmen slid his bayonet out of his tactical vest. "Ladies and gentleman!" he called. "With great pride and honour, I give you Hyena Road!" He slashed with his bayonet and the ribbon fell in two limp halves. The remaining locals watched with unreadable expressions. A single camera clicked. Rilmen put his bayonet away. He turned to Shorty and said, "Well, I'm richer twenty-five bucks. Let's get going."

Rilmen, Shorty, the staff officers, and the close protection team returned to their various LAVs. The ramps lifted up, the gunners took their positions in the hatches, and a moment later Niner Niner Tac began to pull away from the schoolhouse.

Normally Rilmen did the majority of the radio transmissions from his convoy; he liked as many people as possible to hear his voice coming across the net. But in the back of his LAV he didn't even pick up his headset. His baleful eyes just stared into space.

Shorty put on the headset instead. He thumbed his switch. "All stations, this is Niner Niner Charlie. Our tac is on the move. Estimated time to—"

A voice crackled in, cutting him off. "Break break. Niner Niner Charlie, this is Zero. Multiple contacts south of your position. Something is lighting up down there."

# 16

IN THE CHARLIE COMPANY CP, the immediate aftermath of the engagement at the safe house was fairly anticlimactic, even with Operation Open Highway happening around it. Ryan's sitrep had come in not to Pete but to Jenn: *Three Niner Alpha, this is Six-Six. Bravo Delta Kilo has been neutralized. The men he arrived with are rapidly departing. We have lost observation on call sign Ghost.*

*Three Niner Alpha, acknowledged,* Jenn had sent back. *We will send assets to conduct a BDA. In the meantime start your extraction. Out.*

Then Jenn had turned her attention back to her signallers, focusing once again on Open Highway—even though it seemed like the dedication ceremony was burning out quite quickly. The VIPs were certainly not going to appear. Jenn knew where the VIPs were, of course, and under different circumstances she might've been freaked out to know something that General Rilmen didn't. But all that would have to be dealt with later. Right now Six-Six had to be extracted and this whole mess had to be minimized.

Pete stayed in his corner, shaking all over, for as long as he could. Then he stumbled out of the CP into the daylight. He didn't have any cigarettes on him, so he had to bum one from an NCO smoking at a picnic table nearby. Pete thanked the NCO. He held the cigarette to his lips with a trembling hand and inhaled the smoke and held it in his lungs. This all felt like a bad dream. How? he wondered. How couldn't they have seen what he saw? How did everyone just not understand?

"Pete." Pete turned. Jenn had come out of the CP and was coming towards him. She nodded at the NCO on the picnic table. "Take a walk, Sergeant." Without a word, the NCO got up and ambled off.

"Do you," said Pete, "have any goddamn idea what's just happened?"

"Yes, I do," said Jenn. "Ryan had imminent threat toward a civilian. He intervened."

"Yeah. He intervened in something he clearly doesn't understand. For starters, all the Ghost wanted was an honourable death. Ryan took that away from him when he took that shot. But worse, it's all gonna fall down now, don't you get it? With Khan dead, do you know who's going to replace him?"

Jenn crossed her arms under her breasts. "Tell me."

"*I have no fucking idea*," said Pete. He could feel his blood pressure all through his head. He wondered if this was what presaged a stroke. He took a drag, forced himself to calm down a little. "I have no fucking idea, Jenn, and that's the point. All bets are off now."

"For Christ's sake," said Jenn. "Get over yourself. You fight your way, Pete. Ryan is gonna fight his."

Pete sucked in breath to retort. Just then, the duty NCO came jogging out of the CP. He looked around, spotted Jenn, and came bounding over.

"Ma'am," said the duty NCO. "Need you back in there. Our UAVs are picking up a ton of movement south of Hyena. At least two or three different groups of insurgents, twelve in each group, making their way through the grape fields towards the schoolhouse. Niner Niner Tac is already departing, but our guys are still in their cordon, and Six-Six is about to exfil right through there."

Immediately Jenn turned and followed the NCO back into the CP. Pete watched them go. He stood on the gravel, smoking the last bit of his cigarette, thinking for the first time in a long time that he wanted to go home.

- - -

Once again, Six-Six found themselves making their way through dense grape fields, pounded by the unforgiving sun. Hickey was on point, Ryan was navigating, and Tank and Travis were bringing up the rear. They were zigzagging south and then northwest from the saddleback ridge, en route to a rendezvous point with the friendly forces at the dedication site. Ryan estimated that they would need an hour to bash their way through the low ground. Assuming, as always, that nothing went wrong.

Ryan was damp through his clothes and the

collapsed Tac-50 was very heavy on his back, but he was calm. In his mind's eye he kept seeing Khan drop to the ground. Never before had he felt such complete certainty about an engagement. Such peace. *Badal* was served, and he'd been part of it.

They were about a quarter of the way along their exfiltration route when Jenn's voice came over the comms: "Six-Six, this is Three Niner Alpha. Be advised, we are observing multiple dismounted persons moving tactically south to north through your vicinity. Advise you keep your eyes open and avoid contact if possible." Jenn sounded heightened, but not panicked.

"Six-Six, roger," said Ryan, pitching his voice low.

He called a halt and brought the other snipers in close. They were in a shallow gully between an old mud-brick wall and a long, tangled row of grapevines. The air was still and soundless and very hot. There was no pattern of life to be seen, but out here that didn't necessarily mean anything.

"What's up, Warrant?" Tank whispered.

"Apparently there's a lot of bad guys moving

up through here," said Ryan. "They're gonna run right into the LAVs on Hyena Road, but we don't want to get caught in the middle, so let's take it a little slower."

"Taliban?" said Hickey. "Khan's guys?"

"No idea," said Ryan. "Whoever they are, let's not make them our problem. Okay. Let's move."

Six-Six fell back into their formation. They tracked along the mud-brick wall, keeping their weapons at the low-ready. After fifty or sixty metres they came to the end of the wall. Hickey carefully peeked around it. He leaned back and mouthed *clear* to Ryan. Ryan nodded. It was here that they would angle northwest. Thus far the day remained silent.

Ryan gestured for Hickey to carry on. Hickey turned the corner of the wall and took a bound into the next grape field. Ryan started to follow. The instant he turned around the corner of the wall he felt eyes on him. He stopped dead in his tracks, sweat dripping down his face.

Slowly he pivoted, raising his C8, bringing his finger to the trigger . . .

And found himself staring at the Ghost.

The old man was standing in the middle of a

narrow footpath on the other side of the old wall, as if he knew the snipers would be extracting this way. There was nothing about him to suggest he'd been running, and yet he'd covered a great deal of ground quickly. His strange eyes were blazing but his face was otherwise expressionless. Khan's blood was spattered on his face and beard.

Ryan lowered his rifle and put his right hand to his chest. "Salaam alaikum."

The Ghost did not respond.

"Warrant," Hickey hissed, "what's he doing?"

"I don't know," said Ryan.

"Do you think he knows we just saved his ass?"

An image came into Ryan's mind: the Ghost standing his ground outside the safe house, the younger Khan's head at his feet, while the elder Khan cocked the pistol and raised it.

"I'm starting to think," said Ryan, "it might be more complicated than that."

He took a few steps forward. The Ghost watched him. Tank and Travis moved in from behind the corner of the wall. "We can't stay here," Travis whispered hoarsely.

Ryan stopped a few paces in front of the Ghost. He looked at the old man steadily and said, "I took it away from you, didn't I? The way you wanted to go out. Mitchell had you all wrong."

The obdurate features did not soften, but in English, the old man said, "There is danger."

"Yeah," said Ryan.

Travis jogged forward a few steps, fell in beside Ryan. "Ry, we have to—"

Ryan did not hear the shot that killed his friend. One instant Travis was standing there beside him; the next, Travis was being spun sideways into the mud-brick wall, the left half of his face caved in. Ryan stared dumbly. White noise filled his head. Dust and fragments began to spit out of the wall and up from the dirt on the ground. And still Ryan could only gape. *Trav*, he thought.

Something crashed into him from behind, bowled him to the ground. He squirmed sideways. The Ghost had knocked him over and was splayed low in the dirt beside him. Rounds were crashing in overhead, and now the terrible sound of the world was restored. Automatic gunfire, very close, several weapons at least, and someone—Hickey or Tank or even Ryan himself—screaming *Contact!* over the cacophony.

For a seemingly endless moment, Ryan was

paralyzed flat on the ground. All he could see was Travis's face coming apart. It didn't make sense, how could it have happened like—

The Ghost, still prone beside him, leaned forward and smacked Ryan hard on the cheekbone. The old man growled something in Pashto. Ryan didn't understand the words but didn't need to. The meaning was clear.

He looked over his shoulder. Tank was on one knee, putting bursts of suppressing fire down the nearest windrow. One black-clad man was lying dead or wounded in that direction, blood darkening the earth around him. Closer to hand, Hickey was crouched over Travis, trying to empty a packet of QuikClot into the ragged fissure in Trav's face.

"Hickey," Ryan called.

"Ah fuck, Trav," said Hickey. "Come on, man."

Ryan kicked Hickey in the leg. "Hickey! Strip the classifieds!"

Hickey stared blankly for a moment, then nodded. He began digging through Travis's gear for maps and orders and other documents.

"I got fifteen, maybe twenty guys moving over here on the left," Tank hollered. "Two hundred metres!"

Ryan looked. Way down the windrow he could see the shapes of men in black moving laterally, disappearing between the tangled vines. He pointed his C8 and fired a few rounds. Then he thumbed his comms and said, "Three Niner Alpha, this is Six-Six. Contact. Multiple insurgents, one friendly KIA. We're taking effective fire at grid Quebec Quebec 3307 8976. Wait out." He kicked at Hickey again. "Hickey, we'll never fight our way through this shit. Find me something east."

Hickey brought Travis's map right up to his eyes. "I've got a grape hut, fifty metres straight east of here."

"That'll do," said Ryan. Into his comms, he said, "Three Niner Alpha, Six-Six. Trying to break contact, moving to grape hut, will strongpoint from there."

The shooting had stopped for the moment, but Ryan knew it wasn't because the enemy had cleared out. They were just taking up better positions, probably closing in on both sides, exactly as they'd done that day in Haji Baba. Ryan lifted himself to one knee, and then stood up. Tank stepped in next to him, changing magazines.

Hickey was standing with his rifle in one hand and a handful of the classified papers he'd pulled from Travis in the other. In a shaking voice, he said, "Will we leave him here?"

"Never," said Ryan, taking hold of the strap on the back of Travis's vest.

"What about him?" said Tank, nodding at the Ghost.

The Ghost had also gotten to his feet and was watching them.

Ryan let go of Travis's strap and reached down to his hip and unholstered his sidearm. He turned it butt-first and held it out. The Ghost, looking Ryan straight in the eyes, took it from him.

- - -

"Six-Six, this is Three Niner Alpha." Jenn's voice was audibly tense now, even over the net. "Air assets are currently flying overwatch for Niner Niner Tac. We're pushing for QRF support out of Masum Ghar. Hang in there."

The three remaining snipers were moving west along a windrow as fast as they could. The Ghost was with them, and though the limp in his leg was evident, he ran with lithe, predatory grace. Ryan was bringing up the rear, dragging Travis along. He pawed at his comms with his free hand. "Six-Six, roger. Be advised we have a civilian under our protection, call sign Ghost."

A pause, then, "Three Niner Alpha, acknowledged." Ryan could hear what Jenn wasn't saying aloud. *Please, for God's sake, be careful.*

Another ten metres on and they came to a low trellis wall. Beyond the wall was a break in the grape field. Fifteen or twenty paces of open hardpan led to the grape hut Hickey had found on the map. The appearance of the building was humble enough, but Ryan knew the walls could stop an RPG.

The snipers and the Ghost crouched against the trellis wall. "Tank," Ryan whispered. "You and Hickey first. We'll cover. Move now."

Without any hesitation Tank and Hickey vaulted over the wall and made ready to bound for the grape hut. At that moment gunfire ripped from across the open ground, no more than seventy yards distant. Ryan could see a mound of dirt, the top edges of four or five men behind it, gunsmoke lifting in a cloud above them. He propped his C8 on the top of the trellis wall and fired off a burst. Beside him, the Ghost took careful aim with Ryan's sidearm and popped off half a dozen rounds. Out on the hardpan, Hickey and Tank were covering each other: Hickey firing while Tank took a short, diving bound; Tank firing while Hickey did the same. Ryan looked through his sight and saw a Talib lying on the side of the mound, apparently trying to clear a jam from his AK. Ryan took half a second to steady his aim, then he shot the man once in the chest and once in the head.

The Ghost prodded Ryan in the shoulder. He glanced over, saw the old man holding the pistol. The slide was locked back. Ryan nodded and pulled two pistol magazines out of one of his pouches and thrust them at his new comrade. The Ghost jammed one of the mags into the pistol, let the slide move forward, and began firing again.

Ryan looked back over the trellis wall toward the mound. He counted more men now, at least ten. Hickey and Tank had almost finished pepper-potting their way to the grape hut. Tank was in the lead. He got to his feet and lunged for the side of the building . . .

There was a flash of red fire and a geyser of dirt. IED, old Soviet mine, what did it matter? Tank was torn in half. Three metres behind him, Hickey was sent reeling to the ground. Once again, Ryan was left staring, his head filled up with white noise.

The Ghost vaulted over the trellis and sprinted out across the open ground, showing nothing of the limp in his leg. Bullets kicked up dirt around him. Just ahead of him, Hickey had managed to make it as far as the grape hut wall. Bright red blood was pumping out of Hickey's leg. The Ghost grabbed what remained of Tank and continued forward, heedless of the fire coming at him.

The white noise cleared from Ryan's head. He started to clamber over the trellis, knowing already he couldn't haul Travis's body over it. At the top of the low wall Ryan had to let go of Travis's vest. He felt his friend's body slump into the wild grass and dust below. He could not bring himself to look at the ruined face.

Ryan dropped down from the trellis and raced out across the hardpan, firing at the mound as he ran. In the corner of his eye he saw the smoking crater and the pool of gore where Tank had gone down, and rage started to flood through his veins. He fired out the rest of his magazine, not knowing if he'd hit anyone, not caring. The Tac-50 pounded against his back with every step. He felt a sledgehammer-blow to his body armour, just above his abdomen. The round almost took him down but he kept going. Something seared into his hip.

Then he crashed up against the grape hut wall, soaked with sweat, panting for breath. He dropped out his empty magazine and put in a fresh one. From here, they were out of the direct line of fire from the Talibs at the mound. The Ghost was crouched at the base of the wall, with one hand gripping the pistol and the other holding Tank's upper body by the vest. Beside the Ghost was Hickey, pressing down on the hole in his thigh. His pants leg was already red from crotch to ankle, and his face was ashen.

"Follow," said the Ghost.

He scooted along the wall, dragging Tank. Ryan hauled Hickey up and fell in behind the old man. They turned the corner. Here was a wooden door recessed into the adobe—and not fifty metres away were four Talibs, jogging out across the open ground. Ryan dropped Hickey and took hasty aim and shot down three of them. The fourth man dived headlong into a ditch. Meanwhile the Ghost kicked open the wooden door and dragged Tank through. Ryan grabbed Hickey under the arm.

"I'm sorry, Warrant," Hickey said feebly.

Ryan had no words with which to reply. He carried his sniper through the grape hut doorway.

- - -

There were two UAVs covering the area south of Hyena Road. With her hands balled together, Jenn watched on the CP's monitors. The grape hut had been located. It was a lonely little structure in the midst of the vast fields around it. At least twenty insurgents were buzzing like flies around the building.

"QRF is rolling out of Masum Ghar," the duty sergeant reported. "Twenty mikes to Six-Six's location."

Jenn said nothing, her eyes fixed to the monitors.

"Ma'am?" said the duty sergeant. "Air support is still with Niner Niner Tac."

Jenn nodded.

After another almost unendurable second, she became aware of a person close beside her. She pulled her eyes from the monitors. Pete Mitchell had come back into the CP and was sitting down on the edge of a folding chair to Jenn's left. His features were ashen and he couldn't meet her gaze. She had nothing to say to him.

"QRF is seventeen mikes out," the duty sergeant called.

On the monitor, the flies buzzed ever closer to the grape hut.

- - -

*Wheresoever you may be*, the Quran said, *death will overtake you even if you are in fortresses built up strong and high.*

Ah, but this isn't a fortress, the old man thought. It was nothing but a grape hut, and while the walls were sturdy, they would not hold for very long. The wooden door locked from the inside, but the lock was rusty and weak-looking. In the old days, the old man had found himself in situations like this on more than a few occasions. Once in a house in Maywand, once in a cave near Lashkar Gah, and once—yes—in a grape hut just like this. He couldn't remember where that had been, or how it had ended, other than that death had not overtaken him that day, although it probably should have. That day and many others like it.

There was a lull in the gunfire outside, but the Talibs were close. Close enough that the old man could hear the commands they were shouting to each other, even over the ringing in his ears: *You three, fall in on the left! You two, God willing, you will breach the door!*

In front of the old man, the young ISAF soldier was propped against the wall, his face drained of colour, his leg pumping blood. It was almost inconceivable that he'd lived this long. The other ISAF soldier, the one with fire in his eyes, was crouched a few paces away, looking through a chink in the inner corner of the wall. This one had taken a bullet through the side of the leg but was either ignoring it or unaware of it—the old man knew such ignorance of one's own injuries was possible in the height of battle. The old man had been shot in the left shoulder; he was all too aware of the throbbing pain and the blood running down the inside of his clothes.

The young soldier in front of him moaned. The old man reached under his vest and slid out his long, handmade steel knife—the very one he'd used to take off Hamid Wali Khan's head. The young soldier's eyes widened, but the old man cut a long strip of cloth from the base of his shalwar kameez. He knotted it around the young soldier's thigh. Then, using his knife as a windlass, he cinched it as tight as he could. The young soldier cried out. The old man gently shushed him.

Soviets, Afghans, Canadians, Americans, infidels, mujahedeen—all suffered alike. That look of naked anguish on Bashir Khan's face, when his son's head had dropped into the dirt, was the last suffering the old man needed for this life. He longed to see his granddaughters again—to hear their laughter, to see their sly smiles—but he knew he would not. Their own father would have to find them now, inshallah. As for the old man, if death overtook him in this fortress-that-was-not-a-fortress, he would go willingly.

Willingly, but not easily. The lion prowled in his heart yet.

He picked up the young soldier's rifle and settled it into his shoulder.

---

"Three Niner Alpha, this is Six-Six," Ryan sent. "We are still strongpointing from grape hut. Two friendly KIA, one category A casualty. Running low on ammo. What's the QRF status?"

Jenn hastily came back: "Three Niner Alpha. The QRF is fifteen mikes out."

Ryan felt a wave of dizziness pass through him. He knew he'd been shot—it was strangely painless—and he knew he was losing blood. He was dehydrated on top of that. He steadied himself against the wall and peeked out through the little chink. Six black-clad figures raced by, twenty metres out. He could hear them hollering to one another.

"Ry?" Hickey's voice was weak. Ryan had thought he was unconscious. He looked over at the corporal. "Are they coming to get us out of here?"

Ryan started to reply. Then he just shook his head.

"Don't let these savages get us alive," said Hickey. "Please Jesus, Ryan, not alive."

Beside Hickey, the Ghost was crouched at an oblique angle to the grape hut door, holding Hickey's Coyote at the low-ready, waiting with apparent patience. In the far corner were Tank's remains. At some point the Ghost had covered the torso with a broad swatch of burlap that had been lying on the grape hut floor. Ryan turned his own attention back through the chink in the wall.

More Taliban, now in plain sight. He could poke the barrel of his C8 through the opening and take clear shots at them, but there wasn't any point. He needed to save what ammo he had left for when the door was breached.

If he even needed to wait for that to happen . . .

He backed his eye off the chink again, turned around. Hickey's eyes had closed. The Ghost was looking at him. Then the Ghost looked at Ryan and shook his head. *Don't let these savages get us alive*, Ryan thought. He managed a smile. He said something. The Ghost frowned at him, one heavy eyebrow raised, and Ryan said it again.

"*Badal*, Haji Malik."

- - -

"QRF is held up at a culvert," the duty sergeant reported. "They think they see wires, possible IED."

"God fucking dammit," Jenn snapped. She'd been unable to look at the monitors for the last couple of minutes. Keeping her back turned, she keyed her headset. "Six-Six, this is Three Niner Alpha. I need a sitrep."

A pause, then: "Three Niner Alpha, this is Six-Six." In the background, Jenn could hear voices yelling in Pashto. Ryan's voice itself was calm—so calm that Jenn's heart was filled with ice. "Three friendly KIA. Taliban in force on all points. I am requesting fire mission at grid Quebec Quebec 3312 8976."

Pete shook Jenn's sleeve and jabbed his finger at the map. Jenn looked. The ice in her heart turned to dread. "Six-Six—Ryan—no, that's danger close!"

She heard him saying: "Golf Four Romeo, this is Six-Six. Requesting fire mission."

She heard another voice on the radio, one of the artillery officers up at battle group: "Six-Six, this is Golf Four Romeo, send."

She heard herself saying, *"That's right on top of you! Override fire mission!"*

"Do not override," came Ryan's voice. So calm, so goddamn calm.

Bleakly Jenn looked around, as if there were something, anything in the CP that could stop what was happening. All she saw was Pete. His face showed sorrow and recognition, but something else as well. Understanding. Pete understood what Ryan was asking for. She hated him, she hated Pete Mitchell for what he understood.

And, more than anything, she hated herself, because she also understood.

■ ■ ■

"I authorize danger close," Ryan said into his MBITR. "Fire for effect at grid Quebec Quebec 3312 8976."

Outside the grape hut, the voices in Pashto were closer, closer. Only the walls separated them now. The Ghost cocked the Coyote. A dark eye appeared in another chink in the wall, blocking out the sun. Ryan pointed his C8 and fired a single round and the dark eye went away.

The voice of the battle group artillery officer came back: "Golf Four Romeo acknowledging danger close. Fire mission up."

The wooden door thumped violently. The Ghost put a bullet through it and someone on the other side began to scream. Ryan scrambled over beside the old man. He'd lost all feeling in his leg. The old man glanced at him. Ryan smiled. "I'm going to be a father."

The Ghost jacked the bolt on the Coyote and fired through the door again, lower this time, and the screaming on the other side stopped.

"Golf Four Romeo," came the artillery officer's voice. "Shot out. Standby."

Rounds incoming, Ryan thought. How long? Seconds, no more than that.

"Ryan," said Jenn.

"I love you," Ryan sent back. Then he pulled off his earpiece and dropped it on the ground.

Ryan looked at the Ghost. The Ghost looked at Ryan. There was fire in the old man's strange eyes and a smile on his mouth. The grape hut door splintered inward and men came behind it, and Ryan and the Ghost lay on their triggers and there was a terrible shrieking overhead and then there was nothing.

— — —

There was no sound to accompany the images on the monitors. The artillery barrage impacted directly on the grape hut, and for several seconds the entire frame was obscured by dust and smoke. When the smoke finally cleared there was nothing left. Jenn was turned away, her hands pressed over her belly, her eyes squeezed shut, tears spilling down her cheeks. She'd been unable to watch. But Pete had watched. He'd watched the whole thing. He knew those grainy, silent images would be imprinted on his brain for the rest of his life.

# 17

THE BUILDING IN KANDAHAR CITY looked like almost every other building. It was a dun-coloured walk-up with naked, sooty brick-work and dark windows on the second floor. A battered steel door, painted dark blue, faced the sidewalk; the ground floor walls were otherwise featureless. On one side of the building was a garbage-choked canal and on the other side was a long row of identical structures, leading down to the edge of the Sarposa Market. There was nothing—at least from the outside—to indicate that this building was one of many belonging to the late Bashir Daoud Khan.

Around the building, the city had not quite woken up yet. The early-morning sky overhead, not yet clouded with the day's smog, was clear and pale and endless. An old tinker slowly pushed a cart along the quiet street. A boy walked by, herding three goats toward the market. The Afghan cleaner nodded to them, young herder and old tinker alike, as he ambled along the sidewalk.

The cleaner stopped beside the blue door. He adjusted his vest and scratched at his beard.

Pete was watching from an unmarked, dark-windowed Ford Ranger parked on the curb kitty-corner to the building. He lifted a radio handset, keyed the switch, and said, "That's the signal. You're on."

The special forces operators—eight of them, black helmets and black armour plates over their fatigues, customized carbines at the ready—appeared as if out of nowhere. They moved up the sidewalk with startling precision. The young herder saw them and ran for it, his goats scattering, but the operators passed him by. They closed in on the steel door. The cleaner had already made himself scarce. Two of the operators produced a handheld battering ram and held it between them; in an instant the steel door was breached and the operators filed in through the gap and the street went quiet again.

Pete watched, wishing he had a cigarette to smoke. He was well protected here; for every special forces operator he'd just seen going into the building, he knew there were three more in over-watch positions up and down the street.

The passenger door opened and the cleaner hopped in. He said, "It is happening now, Pete."

"Who gave you the tip about this place?" said Pete.

"My uncle."

"Is every single adult male in this country your uncle?"

The cleaner grinned broadly. "Yes."

"Amazing."

"I know . . . Listen, Pete, my friend, I am going up to Kabul for a while."

"You're going to see your family?"

"Yes," said the cleaner. "And Kandahar is too crazy right now."

"Yes, it is," said Pete. "When will you go?"

"As soon as this is finished."

Pete glanced at his watch. He said, "You might have the clocks, but we have the time."

The cleaner frowned. "What does this mean?"

"You never heard it?" said Pete. "It's an Afghan saying. Well, according to Alexander the Great it was an Afghan saying, back when he was trying to run this shitshow. Three years he was here. By the end of it he was drinking heavily. Completely paranoid. Afghanistan had gotten to him. *The horror, the horror*, you know? One night there was a big party, he got into a row with a guy named Cleitus the Black, a loyal friend who'd saved Alexander's life in an earlier campaign. Story goes, Cleitus accused him of certain things and Alexander threw an apple at his head . . ."

Pete trailed off, feeling compressed under a weight he couldn't name, as if the earth's gravity had abruptly increased tenfold. He watched the building across the street. There was still no sign of what might be happening inside. Clearing rooms was a slow and methodical process, Pete knew, even for the special forces. It would be even slower if there were defenders in there.

Of course, the building might also be totally empty, whether or not it had belonged to Bashir Daoud Khan. That was also a strong possibility.

Pete leaned back in his seat. He took off his sunglasses and squeezed the bridge of his nose, hard enough to see a starburst across his vision. A cigarette wouldn't help. He didn't know what would.

The ramp ceremony had happened at KAF the night before, four flag-draped coffins carried one by one into the back of the C-130 that would take them home. As the ramp at the back of the C-130 lifted up, the task force bandsman played the "Last Post" on his trumpet. Five hundred soldiers had gathered to see Six-Six go home, and there was not a single sound among them as the trumpet rang out. Pete had been there, clutching his beret to his chest. He guessed that Jenn Bowman was there somewhere too, but he didn't see her, and he didn't try to find her. Rumour had it she was being taken out of theatre for some kind of medical reason.

Just before the ramp ceremony, General Rilmen had given a brief, muted commentary to a small assembly of journalists, who in turn piped the general's comments to all the major news networks back in Canada. *These snipers died in a security operation in support of the Hyena Road dedication ceremony. Although the road is a great accomplishment here, the deaths of these four brave men serve to remind us of how every victory must come with sacrifice. Lest we forget. Thank you, I won't be taking questions.*

Security operation indeed. As it had turned out, the three groups of insurgents who'd been making for the dedication site had been waylaid by their chance encounter with Six-Six. And after what had happened at the grape hut, no insurgent was left to come anywhere near Hyena Road. Pete didn't yet know what General Rilmen made of that. So far no word had come out of task force HQ about the general's personal feelings—media comments aside—about the whole ordeal. Not even Chewey had any gossip. All Pete could be sure of was that some kind of fallout would come his way. He'd been the one to divert both VIPs from the dedication ceremony, after all, and now both VIPs were dead. Whether a little bit of fallout or a lot was going to find him, he was too exhausted to care.

Elsewhere, it was too early to tell what would fill the vacuum left by Bashir Daoud Khan. Somebody, something, would fall into place. That was certain. But Pete didn't care about that, either. What had happened to Khan was *right*, and in the end, rightness had to count for something.

As for the Ghost, the Lion of the Desert, Haji Malik—what little remained of the old man had been washed and bound in white linen and committed to the earth on a lonesome plain outside Haji Baba. The grave was marked with a small pile of stones. The cleaner had obtained a picture of it through his network of uncles and had given the picture to Pete. Pete vowed he would visit the site if he was ever able. Maybe when this war was over.

"What happened?" said the cleaner.

"Hmm?" said Pete.

"When Alexander threw the apple at the other man's head?"

"Oh. Well, Cleitus accused him of more things. Things that challenged Alexander's honour. So Alexander grabbed a spear and chucked it into his friend's heart. As he watched his friend die he lost his mind. Five years later, Alexander himself was dead."

"This is a sad story, Pete."

"I know it is."

At that moment two of the operators emerged from the breached doorway. Each of them was carrying a little girl in his arms. The girls were bedraggled and dirty and barefoot—but Pete could see them both blinking at the early daylight. Their father, Abdul, was waiting for them in the infirmary at Camp Nathan Smith, only a few city blocks from here.

Pete closed his eyes. The unnamed heaviness still consumed him, but at its edges he felt the first stirrings of relief.

"Was Ryan your friend?" said the cleaner.

"I . . . I don't know. I like to think he was. I don't have too many friends here."

"You have me," said the cleaner. "I'm your friend."

Pete smiled. It felt like it had been years since he had smiled. "Yeah, Haji. You are."